WHAT OTH
ABOUT HENRY AND THIS BOOK

"In this book, Henry talks about how we must become aware of generational patterns so we can identify our tendencies and make intentional choices in light of parental influences. Many of us are not aware that we are *people pleasers,* nor the harm it does to our families. This book helps readers take a deeper look at themselves and is a call to action, reminding fathers of their crucial role in the family and society. I completely relate to *Honor Our Sons*! I especially like how Henry talks about the importance of developing self-awareness and the need to be intentional about life. Overall, Henry helped me to learn about detrimental, widespread father absence. Thank you, Henry!"

~ Alice Benton, PhD

"I can see how men can find themselves in Henry's story and be challenged by what he teaches. There are great benefits to *Honor Our Sons*, and the content is strong! This book takes the reader deeper into the journey of growth in compassion by considering how a man's inner strength can bless others and how the lack of inner strength can wound others. While reading this book, I gained a clear sense of Henry's background, concerns, and hopes for his readers. Even more, I felt drawn into the story as I related my own experiences. I invite you to get to know Henry through *Honor Our Sons* and journey with him into loving your family with purpose and clarity."

~ Darryl Handy, MDiv
Currently a Pastor for Mission Community Church in N.C.

"*Honor Our Sons* chronicles Henry's journey to manhood and how he taught his sons to follow the same path. The lessons are powerful: live a life of integrity, don't obsess about pleasing others, use difficult situations to work on yourself. Henry has given the rest of us a similar blessing, allowing readers to learn from his example. This is a wonderful gift."

~ Ryan Snyder

"Henry painted a picture of what his behavior looked like before and after his men's weekend and intensive counseling. He describes how his behavior changed within his marriage, family, and at work, while showing what it looks like to stand down and stand up. *Honor Our Sons* captures and explores the psychological and social impact of a father's absence. Through learning about Henry's uncertainty as a husband and father, he is qualified to explore this topic. As a father, I am aware of the uncertainty of raising a child. Henry does a wonderful job normalizing this uncertainty and provides a path forward."

~ Brad Fittes, LPCC

"Personal, humbling, often emotional, Henry's story and his vulnerability in *Honor Our Sons* serves as an inspiration for men needing to feast on the roles of leader, father, and man. For men seeking to avoid toxic masculinity, Saas offers an appropriate, spiritual, and manly alternative that bonds the father and son, and the whole family (any definition of family). Saas transitions from memoir to practical application and details his plan and choices to host a rite of passage ceremony for his sons that nods to the traditions of Native Americans, ancient cultures, and the military. This book is about the transparency and community men need to become better citizens and to lead the next generation."

~ J.M. Green, author of *The Novice Angler*

Honor Our Sons

by Henry Saas

HonorOurSons.com

Honor Our Sons

Henry Saas

HonorOurSons.com

Honor Our Sons
A Dad's Story of How He Initiated His Sons into Manhood and How You Can Too

Henry Saas
Copyright © 2021 by Henry Saas.
All Rights Reserved.

Published by: Transform Publishing

All rights reserved. No part of this book may be used or reproduced in any manner whatsoever without written permission, except in the case of brief quotations embodied in critical articles and reviews.

For more information, contact the author at HonorOurSons@gmail.com.

Senior Editor: Allison Rimmele
Developmental Editor: Elena Rahrig
Copy Editor: J.M. Green
Cover Design: Lizzy Dye
Book Layout: Elena Rahrig
Author Photo: Jonathan Saas
ISBN: 978-1-0879-2219-5
ISBN eBook: 978-1-0879-2220-1
LOC: 2021909004
Printed in the United States of America
Every attempt has been made to properly source all quotes.
First Edition

HonorOurSons.com

For my sons:
Tyler Reed
Jonathan David
Jordan Peter

You are amazing men.

HonorOurSons.com

HonorOurSons.com

Contents

Foreword 11
Preface 13
Introduction 15
Men's Weekend 21
The Difference 33
Generational Chains 41
Building a Man Out of a Boy 49
Ingredients for Being a Good Man 69
What Makes a Man? 83
How Do Women Want to Be Treated? 99
Ingredients for Being a Good Father 113
Rite of Passage & Ceremony 141
Building a Team 151
One-on-One Time 155
The Mark of Manhood 163
How I Began 171
Preparation 179
The Weekend with My Sons 185
Reflections 199
Henry's Journal About Tyler's Ceremonial Weekend 201
Tyler's Initiation & Blessing 203
About Tyler 207
Henry's Journal About Jon's Ceremonial Weekend 209
Jon's Initiation & Blessing 213
About Jon 219
Henry's Journal About Jordan's Ceremonial Weekend 221
Jordan's Initiation & Blessing 225
About Jordan 229
Final Thoughts 231
What's Next? 235

About the Author 239
Acknowledgments... 241
Appendix A: Ideas & Insights 247
Appendix B: Important Topics to Talk to Your Son About
.... 249
Appendix C: Ceremony and Rite of Passage Ideas............... 253
Appendix D: Men to Include on My Team 255
Appendix E: Breakfast Agenda for Meeting with Potential
Volunteers 257
Appendix F: Men's Breakfast Checklist 259
Appendix G: Needs Sheet 261
Appendix H: Rite of Passage Schedule.................................. 263
Appendix I: Information Sheet.. 265
Appendix J: Letter to the Volunteers.................................... 267
Appendix K: Roles Explained.. 277
Appendix L: Sons' Packing List... 279
Appendix M: Packing List for Volunteers 281
Appendix N: What I Need to Bring...................................... 283
Appendix O: "What Makes a Man?" Bible Study 285
Appendix P: Intimacy Needs Sheet....................................... 289

Foreword

The first time I met Henry was in a small gathering at work. While engaging in small talk, I asked if he had any children. He replied, "Yes, three."

"Oh, how old are they?" I asked.

"24," he said.

"And…? And…?" I questioned.

Henry loved a good tease. That's when I found out he was the father of triplet boys.

As a mother of two, I know parenting is hard work. Parenthood changed me in unimaginable ways. I quickly began to understand the responsibility I carried for their physical, emotional, and spiritual well-being. I was also their memory maker; and if that wasn't enough, I was responsible for being their role model. *Yikes!*

In Henry's book, *Honor our Sons,* he addresses how to be a good parent which begins with a deep look into oneself. With little guidance from his parents during his youth and into adulthood, Henry worked diligently to secure his blueprint for being a man of integrity.

With triplet sons to teach, lead, and initiate into manhood, Henry realized the teacher first needed to become the student; and so began his journey to self-awareness, personal growth, and the rites of passage. Since then, his passion and focus have been to grow boys into mature men and help men create a vision for mature masculinity.

Whether or not you were blessed with good role models, Henry takes you by your proverbial hand and guides you on a path to maturation and awareness, compelling you to identify

Foreword

and discard toxic behaviors to become who God intended you to be. As Henry's book favors the male perspective, I believe women recognize and appreciate having a decent, strong partner with whom to raise their children.

Through up-close and personal observation, I admire a proactive man who takes responsibility, leads courageously, and has a servant's heart. Henry embodies it all, and I am proud to be his wife. I hope you enjoy his book, *Honor Our Sons*.

~ Deborah Saas

Preface

This book ultimately describes how I held an initiation and blessing ceremony to honor my sons as they transitioned from adolescence to manhood. Before I can take you through the planning, preparation, and execution phases of that ceremony, I must first give you some perspective by sharing my story.

My motivation for writing this book is twofold. First, I want to preserve the events herein for my children and grandchildren. Second, I hope you will read this book and be inspired to intentionally honor the growth of your son(s) into manhood.

As you read *Honor Our Sons*, keep in mind that my definition of manhood may not be your definition, and that's okay. Above all, understand this is the rite of passage I chose for my sons, and I do not expect you to copy what I did verbatim. You must explore what works best for you and your family. *What will be meaningful to your son? What resources do you need? What resources are easily available?*

Finally, I have included supporting documentation at the end of this book. Hopefully, these documents will assist you when it comes time for you to initiate and bless your sons. I encourage you not to get too bogged down in the details. Some details are simply for historic preservation, while others may serve as catalysts for generating ideas on how you can complete an initiation and blessing ceremony without reinventing the wheel.

When I reflect on my childhood, I cannot remember a distinct moment when my dad took me aside and discussed what it means to be a man. I have met many men who don't recall

Preface

having such a discussion with their fathers either, and their behaviors mirror their fathers' with little to no thought of raising their sons differently. My ultimate hope is that my story inspires you to create a new tradition, one of honoring your son into manhood.

Introduction

The National Fatherhood Initiative (NFI), which can be found online at Fatherhood.org, is a "non-profit organization working to end father absence." NFI's website declares, "There is a father absence crisis in America. According to the U.S. Census Bureau, 18.3 million children, 1 in 4, live without a biological, step, or adoptive father in the home. Consequently, there is a father factor in nearly all social ills facing America today." (2020, U.S. Census Bureau. Living arrangements of children under 18 years old: 1960 to present.) The article continues, "Research shows when a child is raised in a father-absent home, he or she is affected in the following ways:

- four times greater risk of poverty
- more likely to have behavioral problems
- two times greater risk of infant mortality
- more likely to go to prison
- more likely to commit a crime
- seven times more likely to become pregnant as a teen
- more likely to face abuse and neglect
- more likely to abuse drugs and alcohol
- two times more likely to suffer obesity
- two times more likely to drop out of high school."

These statistics are astounding as much as they are sad. Moving forward, who has the potential to change the trajectory of our children? Who is to blame for the lack of fathers in the home? Who potentially has the power, compassion, motivation, and patience to put their foot down and say, "Enough is enough"? The answer to those questions is… wait for it… Dad. Dads play an incredibly important role in the lives of their children, for better or worse. It's time we, as men and dads, commit to engaging with and developing our sons.

This book will provide you with answers by giving you tools to be a change agent for your family. You will gain insights into your character, behavior, and thought patterns, so you can identify the ways you contribute to or subtract from honoring your son.

By the time you're done reading this book, you will have learned about yourself and the initiation and blessing ceremony I did for my sons. Hopefully, my story will spark your interest and generate ideas as you start planning to honor your son into manhood.

It's important to note that initiating your son into manhood is directly tied to the depth of your character as a man and a father. Does this direct connection mean you have to start working on yourself before initiating your son into manhood? Quite possibly. Here's why. I would argue that you can't train your son to grow into mature masculinity if you haven't been trained yourself. It's no different than me training someone to be an airplane pilot when I've never been trained as a pilot.

When I finally matured as a man, I felt qualified to train my sons on how to grow into mature men. You may already be well-qualified to train your son. To be sure, I encourage you to ask your wife, trusted friends, and mentors if your character and behavior reflect that of a mature man. Look in the mirror and ask yourself the same question. Are you a mature man, inside and out? Do you have the character required to guide your son wisely?

The direct connection between initiating your son into manhood and who you are as a man is why this book is a journey of self-awareness, humility, transparency, and courage. In the

Introduction

end, you have the potential to be more self-confident, authentic, and intentional. You also have the opportunity to see the benefits of investing in yourself. All of this insight can be yours as you learn the *how* and *why* of creating, planning, and executing your son's initiation and blessing ceremony.

Who I am and the experiences that molded me might be different from who you are and your experiences, and that's perfectly fine. Years ago, when I was 41 years old, I attended a men's training weekend in which I was initiated into manhood. This life-changing weekend was followed by 2½ years of weekly meetings with other men. These meetings allowed me to learn and apply valuable lessons to my life. As a result, my maturation process kicked into high gear, and for the first time in my life, I felt that my internal age matched my chronological age.

I am the first to admit that I don't have a PhD after my name, and I'm not a counselor. However, I have three reasons why it is worth your time to hear what I have to say. First, with over 37 years as a father, I have earned the title of D.A.D. (*Dedicated Active Dad*). I learned, almost too late, how to effectively engage with my sons. In my humble opinion, my wife and I successfully raised three sons from boyhood to manhood. I've been their dad, coach, mentor, cheerleader, critic, and friend.

Second, I have scars on my heart and soul representing my mistakes, people I've hurt, regrets I must live with, and painful life lessons. In short, I have experience with screwing up. Everyone has a story, and I choose to share mine with you in hopes you'll be inspired and challenged to do your best as a man, husband, and father.

Lastly, over the last 25 years, I've participated in and facilitated men's groups that focused on resolving unhealthy behaviors

Introduction

by examining their origin and renewing our efforts to be responsible men. Many men have impacted me in positive ways. I want to do the same for you.

Here are a few notes before you get started. I changed the names of the men within my story because I wasn't able to track the men down to obtain their permission to include them in this book. In addition, my book is intended to be inclusive. If you have a heartbeat, this book is for you. It's worth noting that since this is my story, there will be Biblical references from time-to-time. I believe in the saving grace of God through faith in His Son, Jesus. As you read this book, I encourage you to take what you want to keep and leave behind the parts you don't want.

Are you ready? Are you ready to be the father your children need? Are you ready to be the husband you are meant to be? Are you ready to learn, then teach your son? Are you ready to honor your son into manhood? If so, turn the page.

HonorOurSons.com

PART 1:
Journeying with Henry

HonorOurSons.com

Chapter 1: Men's Weekend

Chapter 1
Men's Weekend

"The only way out is to go in."
~ Unknown

With no clear direction in my life, I was living day-to-day without intention. I got married when I was 21 years old. I was employed full-time, but I had no idea how to be a good husband. Looking back, I was a boy in a man's body for far too many years. I had earned an Associate's degree in Liberal Arts, yet didn't have any direction career-wise. I wanted to be an actor, but my mother told me, "Get a real education, something you can fall back on if acting doesn't pan out." With that advice, I felt like the carpet had been pulled out from under my feet.

Over the next eight years, I stumbled through at least six jobs (maybe more) before landing a job in banking, which turned into a seventeen-year career. Three years into banking, in 1983, my three sons were born. Yes, all three of them... at the same time. Triplets. To make ends meet, I worked full time at the bank, part-time at a local department store, and attended evening classes in business at Arizona State University. However, when it came to my sons, I had no idea how to raise them. Yes, the first year seemed like nothing but maintenance. Eat. Sleep. Poop. Rinse. Repeat. It was a schedule that didn't require a lot of deep thought around what the future held for these three cute babies. However, I quickly learned that babies grow, and

Chapter 1: Men's Weekend

in no time at all, my sons were real people with their own wants and needs. As author, blogger, and speaker, Gretchen Rubin, states, "The days are long, but the years are short."

For the first 12½ years of my sons' lives, I'm sure I taught them some lessons here and there, but these lessons weren't taught with intention. There wasn't a goal in mind about how these lessons might help build a solid foundation for my sons. Overall, I only did what I needed to do to make it to the next day, such as helping them with their homework. I never had a long-term perspective on my sons' lives until *I changed*, until I matured.

I had a few close friends and many acquaintances, but I was the guy who was alone in a crowded room. You wouldn't have known it to look at me because I am an extrovert. Although, if you were able to look inside of me, you would have clearly seen my loneliness. I felt empty in my gut. My dear friend, Diane, and I referred to my emptiness as "a doughnut hole." Something, or many things, were missing in my life. I had no personal and professional goals. I had no conscious understanding of how my choice of words, destructive behaviors, and poor decisions negatively impacted my wife, sons, employees, friends, others, and even myself. I was lost.

Fortunately, two events took place that set me on a path to a fuller life with many blessings. The first event was in 1992. At the urging of my therapist, I took a week of vacation and scheduled twenty hours of counseling over five days to meet with a therapist specializing in marriage and family relationships. During those twenty hours, the therapist and I put my life under a microscope, analyzing every detail. We looked at my childhood, my adolescence, and my adulthood. Even more, we looked at my marriage and the relationships I had with my children, friends, colleagues, and acquaintances.

Chapter 1: Men's Weekend

Sadly, it was the first time I was taught critical life lessons and began to understand relationships and life. As a result, I had a better grasp on the concepts of boundaries, integrity, authenticity, and responsibility. After one particular counseling session, I remember driving to a local superstore. Once I parked and exited my car, I had to cross the two-way traffic area in front of the store. As I crossed, I didn't look for an opening, but instead simply kept walking to the entrance without glancing at the traffic. I didn't have a death wish. My bold behavior was motivated by my feelings of self-worth. As a result of the work I did with my therapist that morning, my self-esteem was off the charts. I thought the drivers would stop for me because it was ME crossing the street. Well, the drivers stopped, of course, but only because I was a pedestrian who wasn't paying attention to traffic. The work I was undertaking with my therapist was rebuilding me from the ground up. I felt so good, not in an arrogant way, rather in an "I matter" way. After 37 years of life, I finally understood that I mattered. If I didn't matter to anyone else, I knew I mattered to God and myself—both are more than enough.

The second event was getting to know Mitch. He and I were colleagues at a bank where we were both branch managers. We initially met during a week-long sales conference the bank held for its top performers. He managed a branch in a city just over 200 hundred miles away. I managed the bank branch in the town he grew up in and where his parents still lived. When Mitch would come to town to visit family, he would always stop by my bank branch to say hello. Frequently, that hello turned into a deep and lengthy conversation. The day came when Mitch invited me to an open house for The Mankind Project and The New Warrior Training Adventure.

Chapter 1: Men's Weekend

The open house was on a Sunday afternoon at an exquisite hotel about 45 minutes from my home. Since I didn't know what to expect, I asked a friend to join me. On the day of the event, my friend called to tell me that he decided not to attend because he was invited to a picnic with his Alcoholics Anonymous group. So, I turned to my wife and asked her to go. As I recall, she wasn't too thrilled with the idea because it meant bringing our twelve-year-old triplet sons, hoping they could sit still through the presentation. However, with some urging—actually begging—she relented.

When we arrived, there were a fair number of people already seated. My wife sat in the back of the room with one of our sons, and I took a seat towards the front with the other two. The stage had thirteen chairs on it arranged in a semi-circle. Right on time, the door opened, and thirteen men walked single file up to the chairs to take a seat. Then, one-by-one, each man stood up and told us what their weekend training adventure meant to them. I was blown away by their transparency, depth of emotion, and the significant lessons they learned all in one weekend. Those who wanted to register for the upcoming training could reserve their spot with a deposit when the presentation was over. I purposefully, and I mean purposefully, didn't bring a credit card, cash, or my checkbook for this exact reason. I didn't want to go, simply because it scared the hell out of me.

It was then I realized it had been four years since I had completed those twenty hours of therapy. I knew in my heart-of-hearts it was time for more work on myself. From listening to those thirteen men, I knew what I had learned from my therapist was just the tip of the possibilities for me. However, I didn't concede; I didn't jump up to sign up. Instead, my wife

Chapter 1: Men's Weekend

and I stepped out onto the patio, and I asked her, "Do you think I should go?" In an instant, she replied, "Hell yes, you're going!" I reluctantly walked over to Mitch and told him that I would send him a check for my deposit.

Ultimately, I developed a thirst for learning more about who I was, how I came to be who I was, and how I fit into the world. Therefore, I was willing to go to a training weekend, even if it meant going while kicking and screaming. Deep inside, I knew I would come out far better than when I went in; but the journey I needed to take required a lot of work.

I instinctively knew the men's training weekend would be a much different approach than my previous twenty hours of counseling. I feared this new journey would require me to look at parts of myself that had never been exposed to light. Even more, I feared the unknown and the shame I would carry when I admitted the truth about myself and took responsibility for my behaviors. *What would others think when they learned the truth about me as a man, father, and husband?* I felt like I'd get into some kind of trouble, much like the fear a child might have felt if he or she were called to the principal's office. I was aware that I was thinking and feeling like a little boy, even though I was in a man's body. I wanted to protect and keep intact the façade I had built around who I was, because that was all I knew. I was perceived by others as likable, funny, upbeat, and outgoing, but I was really insecure, afraid, and lonely. Lastly, there was the lingering question: *How would I integrate my current self with a new and improved self if I came out of this training weekend "a new man?"*

As the training weekend approached, my fear grew. I didn't want to leave home for the weekend. I wanted to stay within the comfort of my home, my routine, and my family. *(Do you hear the little boy in me? I couldn't hear it then, but I certainly do*

Chapter 1: Men's Weekend

now.) Then, I received a call from a man who was associated with the training weekend. We chatted a bit and he gave me carpooling instructions and ended the conversation by saying he looked forward to meeting me.

Suffice to say, I went into the training feeling small and scared. By the end of the weekend, I had gained many insights that I could immediately apply to my life. Leaving the weekend, I felt grounded, confident, and excited to practice my newfound knowledge every day. When I arrived home, my wife and kids instantly knew there was something different about me. When I told them about the lessons I had learned, my wife responded, "Well... we'll see if it lasts."

I was disappointed to hear her say that, although she was justified in doing so because I had let her down numerous times in the past. I had broken her trust in me, before and after we were married. However, this time was different. Her comment fanned the fire in me to implement what I learned. More than ever, I was determined to stay true to my newly developed life's mission statement. I knew companies and organizations had mission statements, but I never considered having one to help direct my life. I was a lost ball with no direction, rolling aimlessly through life. Now, I had direction. Now, I had a concise, memorized response for when I was at risk of losing my way.

My mission is: "To create a world without shame by loving, honoring, and respecting myself and others." If I'm ever faced with a tough choice, if I ever come to a fork in the road, I easily recall my mission statement and use it as my starting point. If I am committed to creating a world without shame, then my decisions will be noble decisions. My decisions should direct me to love, honor, and respect the other person *and myself*. When I come alongside someone in need, I will offer help; I

Chapter 1: Men's Weekend

will listen to friends with an open heart; I will encourage others; I will model healthy manhood; I will honor my wife and my children, and so much more.

Following the training weekend, the I-Group (Integration Group) met weekly. Every man in attendance had been through a training adventure weekend. These men poured into me as I poured into them. I-Group did exactly what the name implies—it supported me in working every day to integrate into my life the lessons I had learned on my training adventure weekend. While the training weekend opened the door to learning and growing, I-Group helped solidify the changes I wanted to make in my life. I finally felt full inside and grateful to God for my personal growth.

The entire experience helped me to deeply understand the importance of my roles in life. For example, how my role as a husband impacted my wife; how my role as a father influenced my sons; how my role as a man affected my community; how my role as a friend impacted those around me; how my role as an employee and manager impacted my employer and co-workers; how all of my roles combined, directly reflected on me and affected my family. Point blank, the decisions I made, the behaviors I exhibited, how I expressed my emotions, and the words that came out of my mouth impacted every aspect of my life and directly reflected on who I was.

So now, with confidence, I can say the same about you. Every decision you make, behavior and emotion you exhibit, and words that come out of your mouth positively or negatively impact someone around you—including yourself. Most of all, what you say and do is a reflection of who you are.

Do you hear what you're saying to your family? Have you noticed the tone of your voice? Are you making noble decisions in your life? What or who do you use to guide your decision making? Do you have a personal mission statement? When you die, what is your legacy going to be?

You're the Captain
My life is like a boat traveling forward in the water. As the Captain of this boat, it's imperative to periodically turn around and see what or who is in my wake. If the water in my wake is smooth and I can't think of anyone I dishonored or hurt, then it's likely I lived in the present—was aware of my tone, words, decisions, and actions.

On the other hand, if I turn around to look at my wake and see the faces of people I've hurt, hearts and promises I've broken, and people I've talked to in an unpleasant tone, then the water in my wake is turbulent and it's time to do two things. First, I need to apologize to the people in my wake and ask for their forgiveness. Second, I must change my behavior. You see, I now try to live my life in such a way that I never have to apologize to anyone for something I've said or done. By being present in the moment, I'm acutely aware of how I treat and serve others. When I do make a mistake, I am the first to apologize and take ownership of what I said or did.

What does your wake look like? After assessing the appearance of your wake, would those close to you agree with your assessment? Are there apologies that need to be made? If you want to smooth out your wake but don't know where to begin, then start by making your brain work faster than your mouth, honor those around you with your empathy, lift people with your words, respect everyone, and be a good listener.

Chapter 1: Men's Weekend

Here's the bottom line... it sucks to grow up. How nice, at some level, it would be to have mommy and daddy take care of you your whole life. As you know, it doesn't work that way. The more responsibility you take on, the faster you mature, and the more you will begin to feel like a man in a man's body. If you want to grow, then learn from my mistakes and triumphs found throughout this book.

Life is a team sport. I have men sitting on the bench waiting for me to call them into the game to assist me in becoming successful or to work through a personal challenge. Likewise, I'm sitting on their bench waiting for them to call me into their game of life. Now I am calling you into the game. It's a serious game that should never be taken lightly. Are you ready to step up? Are you ready to go to the next level of maturity? Are you ready to step into real manhood? Are you ready to win in life? If you're still unsure, just ask your partner. I bet your partner will say, "Hell yes, you're ready!"

HonorOurSons.com

Chapter 1 Exercise

Name a few of your behaviors that are not reflective of being a mature man.

1.

2.

3.

4.

5.

Name a few positive behaviors you would like to incorporate into your life because they would more fully develop your noble character.

1.

2.

3.

4.

5.

Chapter 1 Exercise

Name at least three people who want and need you to be a mature man.
1.
2.
3.

Chapter 2: The Difference

Chapter 2
The Difference

"Everyone thinks of changing the world,
but no one thinks of changing himself."
~ Leo Tolstoy

The twenty hours of concentrated counseling and subsequent training weekend had a huge effect on my day-to-day life. Take something simple, like dining out and having a bad experience. Before the counseling and training weekend, the following account is an example of how the evening might unfold.

My wife would ask, "Henry, where would you like to eat tonight?" To which I would respond, "Wherever you want to go is fine." Arriving at the restaurant of my wife's choice, the hostess would seat us, asking, "Would you like a booth or a table?" My wife would look at me for an answer, and when she didn't receive one, she would respond for the both of us with, "A booth will be fine. Thank you."

Soon enough, the server took our order and delivered our food, we would eat, and then the server returned to ask, "How is everything? Are you enjoying your food?"

Despite the fact my wife had just finished informing me that her food was cold, I would quickly answer the server, "Yes.

Chapter 2: The Difference

Everything is great!" Needless to say, my wife would be terribly disappointed since I ignored her opinion. She would sit poking at her food, barely eating any of it. *I can only imagine what she was thinking.*

After my counseling and training weekend, here is an example of how I would handle the same situation.

My wife asks, "Henry, where would you like to eat tonight?" I respond with, "I am in the mood for Mexican or a good steakhouse. What are you in the mood for?" Then, together, we agree on a place to eat.

Arriving at the agreed-upon restaurant, the hostess greets us, asking, "Would you like a booth or a table?" Knowing my wife prefers a booth, I answer, "A booth will be great. Thank you."

Soon enough, the server takes our order, he delivers our food, we begin eating, and then the server returns to ask, "How is everything? Are you enjoying your food?" To which I respond, "Actually, no. My wife's food is cold. Will you please put it back on the grill for a few more minutes?"

I instruct the server to have my wife's food put back on the grill only because I previously spoke with my wife to fully understand her desired outcome. Did she want her food to be recooked? Did she want to order a different meal? In no way do I take it upon myself to decide my wife's dining fate.

When my wife can see that I'm engaged in our conversation by listening to her concern and desired outcome, acting on her behalf and speaking appropriately with the server, my wife can now sit back assured that I am always looking out for her best interest; and she never has to fight alone. She knows I care about her well-being and live to protect and stand up for her.

Chapter 2: The Difference

She now smiles, and I can only imagine that she's thinking to herself, *my husband has my back*.

Keep in mind, the issue was not whether or not my wife could stand up for herself, because she absolutely could. The issue is whether or not I'm able to speak the truth with kindness to the server. Can I let go of the anxiety that drives me to be a people pleaser, even if it's the server I'm trying to please? Can I overcome conflict avoidance and face the server head-on?

The irony with my first example is that the server is pleased since I told him everything was fine with the food when it wasn't fine at all, but my wife isn't pleased. As a result, I got exactly what I didn't want, a disappointed wife. Why did I care more about pleasing the server instead of my wife? In the second scenario, not only was my wife pleased because I spoke up about her cold food, but the server was grateful for the opportunity to make my wife's culinary experience the best it could be. That's a win-win.

The big questions are: How did I turn out to be a man who sat back and did nothing? How did I become a man without a voice… a backbone… an opinion? How did I become a man who couldn't even stand up for his wife? What type of man was I modeling for my sons?

I was raised with many mantras that led to negative results, although they were meant for good. The one I heard in my head for most of my formative years came from my mom and was "Always say 'yes,' never say 'no,' you want people to like you."

Talk about an unhealthy way to live. Through this message, I learned never to stand up for myself, avoid conflict, and go along to get along—even if there was a cost for doing so. This mindset was one of many aspects of my upbringing that set me up to be

Chapter 2: The Difference

lost, confused, and insecure as a child, adolescent, and adult.

Another example to demonstrate the difference between who I was prior to my maturing as an adult, and who I am now, is in how I used a challenging work environment to deepen my character. In one of my positions, I worked as a manager with seven subordinates. My boss treated all of us with disrespect, going to great lengths to undermine our work. Often, I would walk past my boss in the hallway and give her a greeting of, "Hello" or "Good morning," to which she wouldn't respond or even look at me.

One day, my staff and I were gathered in my cube talking about how poorly she treated us. I chimed in with my two cents, and in that instant, I really heard the words that were coming out of my mouth. At that moment, I recognized I didn't like the man I was presenting to others. I vowed then that I would do all I could to support my boss and encourage my staff. All personal feelings aside, I knew how my boss treated me and others was not about us, but about who she was.

Yes, she was the worst boss I've ever had in all my years of working, but I knew how I reacted to her poor leadership was a reflection of me. She could say and do whatever she wanted, but she could no longer agitate me. I was able to let her be responsible for her actions, just as I was responsible for mine. I knew my legacy as a manager would not include battling with her by giving back what she was giving me. I made a conscious decision to rise above her unprofessionalism.

If I were in that same scenario with my bad boss before my growth into masculine maturity, I would never have been aware that I was participating in gossip with my staff. I would never have been aware that my words reflected poorly on who

Chapter 2: The Difference

I was as a person. I would have hated Sunday nights knowing I'd have to go to work in the morning. I would have brought the anger and frustration I felt in the job home to my family, which they wouldn't have deserved. I would have added to my insecurities through self-doubt. I would have believed my boss that I just wasn't good enough. Finally, I wouldn't have continued to work for her as long as I did because I would have quit as soon as the work environment deteriorated. Instead, I had five years of personal growth by practicing mature masculine decision-making and behaviors. I found it rewarding, and even fun (although I didn't show it outwardly), when I could watch my boss's behavior spiral out of control, and yet I felt peaceful because I could be responsible for only my behavior.

It's going to sound strange, but I use people to my advantage and encourage you to do the same. You see, I used the server to work on myself, help me practice standing up for myself and my wife. I used my bad boss to increase my ability to be patient, further develop my feelings of empathy, and successfully manage my emotions while continuing to do the best job I could, which contributed to my boss's success. Every time she ignored my greeting became an opportunity for me to showcase who I was to myself. Understand, it wasn't important for me to show her who I was because she didn't care. It was important for me to be a grounded man, a non-abusive powerful man, a compassionate man, and a man with depth of character. I didn't need to validate those qualities to anyone but me.

Do you live to prove yourself to others? If so, are you exhausted from it yet? Do you have a difficult time standing up for yourself and your family? If so, how do you think your family feels about you overlooking their needs and desires? If you are not sure, I strongly encourage you to ask them how they

Chapter 2: The Difference

feel when you don't take a stand. Begin making a difference in your family by completing the exercise on the following page.

Chapter 2 Exercise

When was the last time you felt the need to prove yourself to someone, and what was the circumstance?

Do you find it difficult to stand up for your family?

Yes	No

If you answered yes to the previous question, what is getting in the way of you standing up for your family?

HonorOurSons.com

Chapter 3: Generational Chains

Chapter 3
Generational Chains

*"Chains of habit are too light to be felt
until they are too heavy to be broken."
~ Samuel Johnson*

Habits and behaviors can be passed down from generation to generation. These habits and behaviors may be healthy and appropriate practices to continue or they may be unhealthy and inappropriate, and need to stop. One of the best examples of generational chains is expressed in Harry Chapin's song, "Cat's in the Cradle." Chapin's lyrics send a powerful message and teach us what not to do as fathers. If you're unfamiliar with "Cat's in the Cradle," I encourage you to listen to the song.

I don't remember my father intentionally teaching me how to be a man, let alone a husband, father, or friend. The only insight I had into manhood was what I picked up subconsciously by watching my dad live his day-to-day life. When I became aware of the impact I had on my sons as their father, I decided to break the chains of dysfunctional behavior that were seemingly passed down from my paternal grandfather to my father.

My father, John, was born in Budapest, Hungary. I don't know for certain whether my paternal grandfather ever taught my father any important lessons about being a man. I'm guessing he didn't, considering he left the home when my father was a teenager. To the best of my knowledge, Dad came to the United

Chapter 3: Generational Chains

States after graduating high school. He then enrolled in night school, graduating from the University of Cincinnati and earning a Bachelor of Science degree in Industrial Management. His college degree led him to work as an Industrial Engineer.

My dad led an honorable life. He earned a living to provide for his family, took us on camping trips, helped me with homework from time to time, and attended my high school theater and musical performances. I even remember working with him on the occasional home project. Overall, he was a good man.

What I didn't get from Dad were the training and tools I needed to succeed as an adult. It was up to me to find my way. Purposefully or not, Dad distanced himself by volunteering to serve in local community organizations. The vast majority of his time and energy went to the Boy Scouts of America. He served for 41 years, held numerous leadership roles, and was honored with the Silver Beaver Award—the Boy Scouts' highest and most distinguished service award.

Ironically, while Dad may have dedicated his adult life to developing boys into young men, I don't recall any one-on-one training from him at home in this regard. Yes, he tried to involve me in Cub Scouts, Webelos, and Boy Scouts, but Dad was never directly involved as my Den or Troop leader. Maybe Dad was hoping scouting would provide me with the trail markers I was meant to follow into manhood. Quite frankly, I'm not sure—if scouting were to mark my trail, it wasn't something that interested me. I loved my dad. I have no doubt he did the best he could with the tools he had in his fatherhood toolbox.

My mother, Regina (better known as Jean), was born in Cincinnati, Ohio. She had a good sense of humor and fulfilled her motherly duties by caring for me when I was sick, driving me

Chapter 3: Generational Chains

to extracurricular activities, helping me with my homework, cooking meals from scratch, and seeing to it that our family attended religious services. Like Dad, she graduated from the University of Cincinnati. She then went on to become an elementary school teacher. For the most part, Mom didn't work outside the home while raising my three siblings and me, but she did do an extreme amount of volunteer work. She volunteered at her local classical radio station for forty plus years. In addition, she volunteered with local community theater and vocal groups. My mom was a pianist and attended every scheduled rehearsal and performance. These commitments kept her out of the house most evenings and many weekends. Therefore, she was physically and emotionally detached from me. It wasn't until she was in her early sixties when she first said, "I love you," to me. I don't know why it took her so long to verbally express her love for me.

Mom often behaved in ways that worked to stifle my emotional growth and damage any self-worth I may have had. She talked baby-talk to me and treated me like I was her little boy, even into my early forties. I have often wondered if her motivation behind baby-talk was to keep me as her little boy so she wouldn't have to admit she was aging. Or perhaps, she needed to feel needed, and if I remained small, she would need to care for me. Maybe she desired a deep connection with me since she and Dad weren't in the happiest marriage. My siblings and I joked how mom and dad only saw each other when they needed to attend, as a couple, their respective volunteer organization's annual Christmas party. Whatever was motivating Mom, I finally put an end to the baby-talk by telling her she needed to treat me as her adult son, or I wouldn't be able to have a relationship with her. To her credit, she stopped talking baby-talk to me.

Chapter 3: Generational Chains

Then there were the years of never being good enough and feeling as though I didn't matter. Mom's modus operandi was to focus on the opposite of any given situation. For example, if I grew my hair long, she'd tell me she liked it better short. If I got a short haircut, she told me she preferred it longer. If I lost weight, she'd caution me not to get too thin. If I gained weight, she'd caution me not to get heavy like Dad.

Mom treated my sister and younger brother in various dysfunctional ways, some were similar to what I experienced, and others were different. My oldest brother, who is the first born and six years my senior, seemed to avoid much of what the rest of us were dealt. In many ways, Mom didn't make it any easier for me to find my way into manhood. I don't mean any disrespect to her. I have no doubt she did the best she could with the tools she had in her motherhood toolbox.

On the brighter side of my mother, she was kind enough (at my request) to write me a letter about myself. Mom was 75 years old at the time, and I was 42. As you may recall from chapter one, my aspiration as a college freshman was to be an actor, but my mother told me to get a real education first. Here is an excerpt from her letter to me that was written 24 years after she told me not to major in theater.

> *"I still have a feeling of guilt for not sending you to [the University of Cincinnati] College-Conservatory of Music's theater department. Instead, I urged you to get an education in a field other than theater so you'd have something to fall back on, then go into theater. Well, theater is an education and I think you would have made it big. It's too bad that life doesn't give us a second chance to do things differently or better. In hindsight, your dad and I can see some of our errors, but we tried to do the best we could at the time."*

Chapter 3: Generational Chains

So how did I learn to be a man? My first step was forgiving my parents for their shortcomings. (Just as I want my sons to forgive me for mine.) Next, I learned by observation, making tons of mistakes, counseling, the training adventure, the I-Group, and listening to my wife. All-in-all, I guess you can call it on-the-job training. As a result of the array of messes I found myself in, I became determined to break the generational chains of silence and the distance between father and son. To that end, I wanted my sons to remember the moment when they made their especially important transition from boyhood to manhood.

I encourage you to take time to self-reflect about the man you are now compared to the man you want to be. Begin now by completing the exercise on the following pages.

HonorOurSons.com

Chapter 3 Exercise

How did you learn to be a man?

What role did your mother and father play in your maturing process?

Chapter 3 Exercise

Do you think some generational chains need to be broken so you don't pass them down to your son?	
Yes	No

If you answered yes to the previous question, what generational chains do you think need to be broken?

1.

2.

3.

4.

5.

How would you rate your maturity level as a man, with one being low and ten high?

1	2	3	4	5	6	7	8	9	10

Are you the man you truly desire to be? If not, what do you think is holding you back?

Yes	No

Chapter 4: Building a Man Out of a Boy

Chapter 4
Building a Man Out of a Boy

"If you want to change the world,
go home and love your family."
~ Mother Teresa

Dr. Michael Obsatz, in his 2003 article titled "From Shame-Based Masculinity to Holistic Manhood," states, "Millions of boys are shamed into fitting into a model of masculinity." Unfortunately, shaming happens every day. Boys are teased, humiliated, and bullied until they learn to modify their behavior to fit in so the hazing will stop. The downside of behavior modification is, not every boy wants to fit into society's masculinity model. Yes, schools and organizations throughout the country are making inroads to curb bullying; however, shaming and bullying doesn't only happen at school.

In an attempt to build a man out of a boy, some dads, moms, and stepparents, knowingly or unknowingly, belittle their sons. Dads, in particular, can inflict deep emotional and long-lasting harm on their sons. Dads who physically push their sons around and tell them to, "Toughen up" or scold their sons for crying with words like, "Suck it up," "Men don't cry," or "Be a man" are just some of the unhealthy messages boys are given. Some other one-liners boys may hear are:

Chapter 4: Building a Man Out of a Boy

- You're not a man unless you can hold your liquor.
- You're not a man until you get laid.
- The more girls you conquer, the more of a man you'll be.
- Real men don't do laundry, dishes, or cooking.
- Real men drink beer, watch sports, and play video games.
- Manly men watch porn.

Spouting these one-liners to your son certainly develops his character, but not in a way he can be proud of. It's neither positive, uplifting, supportive, nor healthy for him—short-term and long-term. Yes, he will physically grow up, but he will remain a boy on the inside.

Are there messages you've been giving to your son that you now realize may not be the best strategy in raising him into a man? If you're not sure, check with your partner. Wives can typically see what we can't—wives know. The good news is, it's never too late to change your message.

So how do you, as a father, fix the complex issues facing your son? How do you grow your boy into a man? First, it's about how you interact with your son on a daily basis. If you truly desire to raise your son into a decent, self-confident man, then you must engage with him.

To maximize the effectiveness of the engagement or communication you'll have with your son, seven attributes (learned skills) need to be part of your character and skill set. Before I give you these seven attributes, remember your behaviors speak louder than your words. Unless I have a solid history with a man built on trust, I rarely take a man at his word; instead, I take a man at his behaviors. Sons will do the same. When your words match your behaviors, you are hitting the bullseye.

If, after reading the seven attributes and skills, you sit back and say, "That's me!" it's best if you consult your wife, partner, or close friend, to confirm your assessment; or even more importantly, ask your son. Similar to what I said earlier, wives, partners, friends, and children know. You just don't want to end up fooling yourself. If it turns out that you're already communicating in all the proper ways, well done!

Attribute #1: Be Humble

Some dads believe they must always be "over" their son, much like a boss over an employee. Ultimately, lording over your son shows a lack of humility. You'll be surprised how close you and your son will become when you change the humility dynamic. I'm not saying to be his bud. (Although, there may come a time for that when he's a grown man.) I'm suggesting you show your son respect by displaying humility. Some examples of humility are listed below.

- Accept when you are wrong and apologize.
- Be a good loser in competitions.
- Be willing to serve others.
- Be willing to perform the most menial tasks—tasks you judge to be beneath you.
- Avoid boasting.
- Avoid the need to be right.
- Listen intently without needing to share your story.
- Listen with the intent not to fix, but to support.
- Before giving advice, ask if your advice is wanted.

When you listen effectively to your family, you can learn much about who they are and their current challenges. You can begin by committing to not talking down to your son. Give him your

Chapter 4: Building a Man Out of a Boy

time and patience, accompanied by good eye contact and encouraging words. Staying present and connected to your son can help you put yourself in your son's shoes and recall how your dad interacted with you. Hopefully, by accessing your memories, you'll know how to be and how not to be—what felt good to you, and what didn't. To organize your thoughts on the matter, take a moment to complete the exercise below.

I accept when I am wrong and apologize.			
Never	Sometimes	Frequently	Always
I am a good loser during competitions.			
Never	Sometimes	Frequently	Always
I am willing to serve others.			
Never	Sometimes	Frequently	Always
I am willing to perform the most menial tasks—tasks I judge to be beneath me.			
Never	Sometimes	Frequently	Always
I avoid boasting.			
Never	Sometimes	Frequently	Always
I do not feel the need to be right.			
Never	Sometimes	Frequently	Always
I listen intently without needing to share my story.			
Never	Sometimes	Frequently	Always
I listen with the intent not to fix, but to support.			
Never	Sometimes	Frequently	Always
Before giving advice, I ask if my advice is wanted.			
Never	Sometimes	Frequently	Always

Chapter 4: Building a Man Out of a Boy

Now that you have completed the exercise on the previous page, are you willing to commit to making the necessary improvements so you can model humility for your son?

You can test your humility. If you are not a man of faith, ask your friends, family, or trusted co-workers if you are humble or arrogant, and have them follow up with examples. If you are a man of faith, submit to God through prayer. Find a private place where you can be alone for fifteen minutes. Then, if you are physically able, get down on your knees and pray. If you are not willing to kneel to pray, spend time reflecting on what's getting in the way of you performing this act of humility.

Humble yourselves, therefore, under God's mighty hand,
that he may lift you up in due time.
1 Peter 5:6 (NIV)

If you decide to commit to praying as an act of humility, be sure your heart goes with you. Yes, I know where you go, so goes your heart; but if you pray and your heart isn't involved, then pray your heart would join you at a future prayer session. Your prayer can be even more powerful if you invite your spouse to pray with you. At some point, think about praying with your son.

It's **H**umbling, **I**ntimate, and **P**owerful. It's **HIP!**

Attribute #2: Be Transparent

Sharing your life with your son while keeping it age-appropriate will fill your son with confidence, and he'll see you as the flawed human being you are... as we all are. Sharing your life is not always about "Today I went to work, went out to lunch, had two meetings in the afternoon, and then came home." It's sharing your *heart* with him. "I felt fear going into a meeting

Chapter 4: Building a Man Out of a Boy

today." "I felt loved by your mom when she called me at the office today just to say hi."

I know society says that real men don't share their hearts with anyone because they don't have one. But I know something about men, *all men*, that you may not know. Every... man... has... feelings. Shocking, I know. So much of life and intimacy is squandered when men hide, repress, and deny their feelings.

At some point, every man has felt some of what I have felt. Mad. Sad. Fear. Shame. Guilt. Pride. Lonely. Peace. Love. Joy. Satisfaction. Ironically, anger is often the only emotion that seems acceptable to show while keeping the other emotions hidden. Society may lead you to believe that if you were to share your heart—your feelings—with another man, he would think you're weak or gay. The truth is, being able to share your heart with another man is a sign of strength. If you don't believe me, ask your wife, partner, or religious leader. They know.

If you apply emotional transparency to the relationship you have with your son, the outcome will amaze you. In my experience, sharing my heart with my sons didn't cause them to run away from me; rather, my sons drew closer to me.

Attribute #3: Be Honest
Being honest doesn't take a whole lot of explanation. Simply put, never lie to your son. If you can't tell him the truth about something, don't make something up. Tell him, "I can't tell you right now." Honesty is the best policy.

Attribute #4: Be a Man of Integrity
Merriam-Webster defines integrity as, "a firm adherence to a code of especially moral or artistic values." You may have a slightly different definition. My definition of integrity is,

Chapter 4: Building a Man Out of a Boy

"a crystal-clear awareness to make sure my words match my behaviors, and my behaviors match my words." This definition demands that I be a good listener to what I say, so there is no difference between what I say and what I do.

Let me give you an example. If I tell my son that I will pick him up to take him to soccer practice at six o'clock, I need to be there at six o'clock. Meaning, I must work backward from the time of my commitment. If it typically takes 45-minutes to drive home from work, I need to leave work at 5:15. However, I must consider all things that may cause me to be late—unusual traffic or weather. Knowing there might be a fifteen-minute delay, I must then leave at 5:00 instead. My commitment also requires me to complete my work by 4:45, knowing it takes time to walk to my car and someone may stop me along the way to chat.

The process of working backward from your commitment time is what I call *Big Bang Thinking (BBT)*. I'm sure you've heard about getting the biggest bang for your buck. Well, BBT is being able to calculate your odds of success with intentional thinking while understanding what's at stake. BBT can get you, and others, the biggest bang in life.

Big Bang Thinking allows for the following to be created. First, it creates a man of high integrity. You are able to live up to the commitments you make to your son. You allow your son to see your character's depth, and witness how your words match your behaviors. Second, it creates patience. For example, you won't drive like a maniac. You won't feel frustrated or angry at other drivers and yell at the car in front of you. You will truly be happy and in a great mood when you pull into the driveway, greeting your son with a hug and the affirmation, "It's great to see you. I couldn't wait to be with you. Let's go to soccer."

Chapter 4: Building a Man Out of a Boy

Third, and this benefit is the big bonus that can't be overemphasized, it creates self-importance in your son. He will know he matters to his dad—which helps him stay out of counseling when he's in his 30's or 40's. (I know I don't want to be the topic of discussion between my son and his therapist. I hope you don't want to be the topic of discussion with your son and his therapist, either.)

You might find my perspective on integrity over-the-top and too much of an effort; I can't fault you for that line of thinking. The main point for you, as a man, is to have high integrity. Yes, you will find things happen that can get in the way of you keeping your word. When it happens, make the phone call. Call whomever you need to inform them of the delay, and do it as early as possible so they can adjust accordingly. A phone call goes a long way in helping others manage their expectations and keeps them from guessing what happened to you, while helping you remain a man of integrity. I encourage you to begin seeing your words and behaviors as a reflection of your character.

Here's a more humorous, exaggerated perspective to show that being a man of integrity can be displayed in all realms. If I tell you I'm a thief and then steal your wallet, I am still a man of integrity. If I tell you I'm not a thief and don't take your wallet, I am still a man of integrity. But... if I tell you I'm not a thief and then take your wallet, I'm out of integrity.

Perhaps this story will hit close to home for you. Unfortunately, there was a time when integrity wasn't even in my vocabulary. I never thought about it nor reflected on what it meant. One recurring example was that dreaded call from my wife just a little after 5:00 each workday. "Honey, what time will you be home for dinner?" or, "Honey, can you be home for dinner at 6:00?" There I was at work dealing with a

Chapter 4: Building a Man Out of a Boy

customer who walked in right before we closed, or I had an employee who needed to discuss an issue with me that couldn't wait until tomorrow, or I justified being late because I wanted to avoid my wife, since we hadn't been getting along, or, or, or… you get the point. To appease my wife, I would tell her I'd be home whenever she expected me that day.

Did I typically get home by the time I agreed to be home? Nope. What message was I sending my wife and sons? What did my behavior say about me—my character? Would my wife and sons think of me as a man of integrity, as a man of my word? Could they count on me? Did I just silently permit my sons to act the same way I had acted towards them? To my wife and sons, I was saying, "You're not as important to me as my work. You can't trust me at my word." By the time I would arrive home, my wife and sons had usually already eaten. They grew tired of waiting for me; my wife was angry, and my sons were disappointed and disinterested in me.

What will the consequences be if you don't keep your word? I want the best for you, your son, your partner, and your family. Do you want your wife, your son and his wife, your grandchildren, co-workers, friends, neighbors, community, country, and the rest of the world to know they can count on you doing what you say you're going to do?

Attribute #5: Be Consistent

My sons, and probably your son, do best in life when there is structure and consistency. How I wish I could have been consistent with my behaviors. I've had way too many missed opportunities. If your son's messy bedroom makes you angry, don't allow the messy bedroom to fester for a month until you hit your breaking point. If you expect chores to be done before

Chapter 4: Building a Man Out of a Boy

you get home from work, make it known to your son—hold him accountable daily, instead of reaching a place of *enough is enough*—your boiling-over point.

Inconsistent leadership creates confusion for the rest of your family. Your unpredictable behavior leaves them walking on eggshells, never sure of how to satisfy you. Will you be okay one day with a messy bedroom, but then the next day scream and dish out punishments? Ultimately, your family will be in a state of continual unrest as they live in fear of your next move. Remember, your family counts on you to lead... leaders are consistent.

Attribute #6: Be a Positive Role Model
Take a minute to think of someone in your life, past or present, for whom you have a lot of respect. This person could be a teacher, coach, sibling, parent, friend's parent, religious leader, spouse, etc. Also, this person likely taught you, formally or informally, at least one important aspect of life you didn't already know. Or maybe they came alongside you to offer their support during a difficult time. Whatever the case may be, these people are the types of folks you will want to watch closely and study. I strongly encourage you to take as much as you can of their good traits and wisdom and apply them to your life.

In his book, *The 7 Habits of Highly Effective People*, Stephen R. Covey puts forward "Habit 2: Begin with the end in mind." Covey's approach to this Habit helped me visualize my own death and grasp the fact that one day I am going to die. I still keep that reality in the forefront of my mind so I can use it to motivate myself to be a noble, outstanding role model—the type of person my sons would want to emulate. This way, at the end of my journey—my funeral—hopefully, my sons

Chapter 4: Building a Man Out of a Boy

would be honored to say a few good words about their dad. Their eulogy wouldn't be obligatory words of sympathy, rather authentic words describing my character's depth and the positive impact I had on them.

How cool would it be to have your son stand at your funeral service and, through tears of sadness, proudly tell everyone that you were his dad, friend, and role model? Can you picture it? At your funeral, your son modeling the best of who you were because you thought it important enough to become a role model for your son, family, and community. That's powerful!

If you can't visualize your funeral, it might be time for you to take a hard look at where you're going in life, how it's going to end, and who will care. Truly, it depends on you, your character, your decisions, your integrity, your behaviors, and more. Beginning with the end in mind was and still is a big motivator for me to treat my sons with respect, pour into them, encourage them, challenge them, help them succeed, love them, and guide them into manhood.

Attribute #7: Be Intentional
If the long-term goal is to successfully transition your son from a boy to a man, you must be intentional. You must be awake. Your eyes must be open. You must be present and engaged. You must be one step ahead of your son. Understand, you have the experience and hindsight that he has not yet acquired.

Look for opportunities to honor and bless your son with a mini rite of passage. For example, if he's going on a date (with his first date being of the utmost importance), be sure to schedule time with him a day or two in advance for the two of you to talk. Your conversation will be the perfect time for you to express your love for him; tell him how proud you are of him;

Chapter 4: Building a Man Out of a Boy

remind him that you're there to encourage him; answer his questions. It's also a good time to teach him that growing into a man involves taking on more responsibility, and taking someone out on a date, treating them with respect, and keeping them safe is just that, more responsibility.

Your son may feel embarrassed by this conversation, but I encourage you to push through and, if you want to, acknowledge any embarrassment. If you have a story from your own life where you felt embarrassed due to the subject matter, this moment would be a great opportunity to share it with your son.

Discuss what he might expect, how the date might go, what challenges he might face, how to treat his date, and what to do if he needs support during the date. If you let your son go blindly into this date, he will surely flounder. He'll find friends to model himself after, or he'll simply guess when it comes to knowing what to do or not do. Sometimes we, as dads, put ourselves on a pedestal, making it below us to have these types of talks with our sons. Also, too often, our sons view us as perfect. As a dad, your job is to outfit your son with the wisdom and tools he needs to complete a date successfully.

The goal is to build into your son—develop him—by honoring, respecting, and teaching him. The template described above for a date can be used for mini rites of passage with a few modifications for each event. Other mini rites can include his transition into high school, the earning of his driver's license, his first time shaving, his first dance, first kiss, going to college, going to his new job, and more. Be ahead of the game. Anticipate what's coming his way as he ages. If you need more information on the different stages of a boy's life and their accompanying characteristics, spend a little time researching the subject online, in your local library, or your favorite bookstore.

Chapter 4: Building a Man Out of a Boy

Celebrating mini rites of passage doesn't have to be a big ordeal. It could be a fifteen-minute or less conversation just between the two of you. Maybe you will want to include his mother. It will be important to prep his mom before the conversation takes place. Some moms want to "mother" their son during his teenage years by not allowing him to take on more responsibility i.e., performing tasks he should be doing himself, not allowing him to make his own decisions, and overly protecting him from life's consequences—not allowing him to fail. However, doing so can stifle his growth into manhood.

It's critical for you, as a father, to get engaged and start behaving as if it matters—because it does! Did it matter how your dad engaged with you? Did he engage? Did he pour the best of himself into you? Did he teach you about life, or did you have to guess at it? Did he respect you along the way? How did you learn to be a man? Did you learn to be a man from your friends? Please, please, please, for all our sakes, don't shame your sons into manhood. Stop working too many hours. Put down your phone. Get off the computer. Quit drinking so much. Stop raging at your family. Stop isolating. Stop avoiding. Stop whatever you're doing that isn't productive and isn't geared toward building a strong foundation for your family. It's time for a change!

You can attempt to justify doing nothing by telling me that you don't know how, or you don't know where to start. But as Wayne Gretzky said, "You'll miss 100% of the shots you don't take." Honor your son, support him, encourage him, believe in him, and, most importantly, let him see and experience a dad who is the best kind of man he can be. Your son's success as a healthy adult male depends on you!

Chapter 4: Building a Man Out of a Boy

Think of the trickle-down effect from generation to generation. If you're a great dad, your son will more than likely be a great dad. In short, if you start now, generations can be impacted in a positive manner. Don't wait. Time is short. If you didn't have a great upbringing, if your dad wasn't fully present or didn't teach you about life, how did that work out for you? Isn't it time for you to break the historically accepted chain of behaviors in your family? What's at risk if you step up? What's at risk if you don't step up?

Do something totally different. Invest in yourself, even if that means spending time with a trained therapist, so you, in turn, can invest in your family. You can do this! Even though we don't know one another, I believe in you because I invested in me and learned to believe in myself. If I can do it, there is no doubt in my mind you can, too.

Chapter 4 Exercise

Do you feel like a boy on the inside? If so, what do you believe contributes to those feelings?	
Yes	No
Are you spending hours playing video games?	
Yes	No
Have you been in fights to prove your masculinity?	
Yes	No
Do you drink too much alcohol or use recreational drugs as a means to fit in or cope?	
Yes	No
To prove you can handle your liquor better than your friends, have you participated in drinking contests?	
Yes	No

Chapter 4 Exercise

Do you watch porn?	
Yes	No
Have you bragged about your sexual conquests?	
Yes	No
Does helping with household chores make you feel like less of a man?	
Yes	No
When you are with your friends, do you participate in bullying others?	
Yes	No
What are three things you must stop doing in order to raise your son into a well-respected, self-confident, successful man?	
1.	
2.	
3.	
What are three time-sucking activities you do that distract you from spending more time with your son and other family members?	
1.	
2.	
3.	

Chapter 4 Exercise

What are three things you are doing correctly in raising your son into a man that you want to commit to continue doing, and maybe do even better?

1.

2.

3.

As you move through this book, use Appendix A to record new ideas you can consider implementing to help transition your son into a man.

HonorOurSons.com

HonorOurSons.com

PART 2:
Learning to be a Man

HonorOurSons.com

Chapter 5: Ingredients for Being a Good Man

Chapter 5
Ingredients for Being a Good Man

"What is a man? For young men, you can't become what you can't define."
~ Dr. Robert Lewis, Pastor

Where there is no vision, the people are unrestrained...
~ Proverbs 29:18 (NASB)

In 2007-2008 I was the Director of Men's Ministry at my church. That year I taught a program to men of the church called *The Quest for Authentic Manhood*. At the time, this program was one of three programs created by Dr. Robert Lewis (a Pastor in Little Rock, Arkansas) under the name *Men's Fraternity*. In his program, the four tenets Dr. Lewis uses to describe manhood are:

- Reject Passivity
- Accept Responsibility
- Lead Courageously
- Expect God's Reward

You can check out Men's Fraternity Classic and 33 The Series (the new Men's Fraternity) at www.AuthenticManhood.com

Chapter 5: Ingredients for Being a Good Man

Thirteen years after my triplet sons were born, I finally, and thankfully, learned many more ingredients that go into being a good man in society. If I had to give you a concise description of how to be a good man, it would be to be powerful and compassionate without being abusive or domineering.

> *"I am not interested in power for power's sake,*
> *but I'm interested in power that is moral,*
> *that is right, and that is good."*
> ~ Martin Luther King, Jr.

Consider the following four ingredients to being a good man. This list is by no means exhaustive. I use slightly different descriptors for what a real man is because there is much that goes into being a good man. Maturing takes hard work and there are many characteristics to consider. Be patient with this process. The journey is not a short trip around the corner and back.

Ingredient #1: Being Responsible
I, unfortunately, didn't mature into a man until I was forty-one. One of the contributing factors to my maturity was my decision to take on more responsibilities. For years my life was lived on Easy Street, not from a financial perspective, rather from a responsibility perspective. I had a job and I cut the grass. *What more was there for me to do?* As it turns out, *a lot*.

My wife did the heavy lifting when we first got married and far too many years after that. She paid the bills, kept the checkbook balanced, shopped for the groceries, cooked, had a full-time job, worked to keep the house clean, and more. Yes, I contributed here and there from time to time; I wasn't a total dud. However, it wasn't until I "woke up" when I started to change. Looking back, I believe it was the culmination of many things: counseling, nagging from my wife, and a thirst to know

Chapter 5: Ingredients for Being a Good Man

more about who I was and why I was the way I was, which motivated me to step up—to take on more responsibility.

The more I dug into my childhood and understood the root causes of my behaviors, belief system, and thought processes, the more mature I became. Once I understood the *why*, the easier it was to decide to change to a healthier me.

In my early twenties, when I first got married, my wife would tell me to hang up my pants and shirts and put my things away, to which I spent many years classifying her directives as nagging. When she nagged, I would become defensive. But then I had an awakening. I can't tell you what initiated the awareness, but suddenly, it dawned on me that maybe my wife was trying to make me a better man.

Look at the facts: she loved me, married me, had my best interest in mind, and wanted the best for her and our children. Maybe, just maybe, her nagging wasn't really nagging at all. Perhaps she was pointing out the life skills I lacked. What if I were to stop getting defensive when she "nagged" me and just implemented the life skill she was teaching me at that moment?

I think I hear the women readers saying, "Duh!" I get it. As I have witnessed, a woman often knows more about her man, and men in general, than men do. When I started listening to my wife and taking action on her "nagging," my life improved. I found the more responsibility I could take on, the faster I matured, and the more I felt good about who I was. I could even feel myself throw back my shoulders and walk a little taller. One unseen benefit that came with my taking on more of the family responsibilities was my wife could relax a lot more. I got the sense she breathed a huge sigh of relief and softened in the process of me helping to carry the load. She no longer had to do it all herself—she now had a partner.

Chapter 5: Ingredients for Being a Good Man

Ingredient #2: Being Respectful
Prior to my "awakening" as a man, I didn't think about how I treated people, particularly my family. Making a sarcastic remark or poking fun at someone in hopes of being funny was commonplace. It never entered my mind to be intentionally respectful to everyone with whom I interacted. Once my eyes opened to the impact I had on another human being, my words and behaviors took on a whole new meaning. I began to realize my words and behaviors can tear someone down or lift them up. I could choose to listen empathetically to someone else's story, heartache, and frustration, or I could make it all about me by cutting them off and telling them my struggles. I quickly changed my mindset and began listening more, paying attention to what I said, the tone in which I said it, and what I did.

What's your story when it comes to respecting others? Do you get caught up with the guys at work and tear down, make fun of, or bully co-workers? If you hear or see someone being disrespected, do you step in to bring it to an end? Do you respect your wife or partner as much as you respect your friends or a stranger? Are you a good listener? When it comes to your children, do you respect them as much or more than you respect someone else's child? Are your words, tone, and non-verbal communication supportive, empathetic, and sincere?

Ingredient #3: Being Reliable
Have you ever had a friend or family member who was unreliable? If so, what do you think about that person who let you down? Don't you expect reliability from others, especially when they make a commitment to you? Have you ever been stood up? Do you know of someone who is always running late? Do you ever feel angry, disappointed, or sad when your friends or family aren't reliable?

Chapter 5: Ingredients for Being a Good Man

Well, anger, sadness, and disappointment can be three prominent feelings someone else feels when you aren't a reliable man. These feelings are exemplified in the typical story of the *son sitting on the porch with his baseball glove and ball waiting for his dad to come home, but Dad never shows up before bedtime.* Your son doesn't care about your excuses. He only cares if you arrived when you said you'd arrive and did what you said you were going to do. Your son has every right to feel angry, sad, and disappointed. It is also the classic story of the *spouse or partner waiting to be romanced but is never invited out for a date night, never given a reason to get dressed up.* Your spouse or partner has every right to feel angry, sad, and disappointed. The consequences of your decisions can be wonderfully positive, or they can be equally disappointing.

I am reliable.			
Never	Sometimes	Frequently	Always
I show up when expected or needed.			
Never	Sometimes	Frequently	Always
My wife and children can count on me.			
Never	Sometimes	Frequently	Always

Ingredient #4: Being Real

This ingredient can be scary. There can be a lot of fear associated with being real because being real is all about dropping your façade, getting rid of the smoke and mirrors, and removing your mask. Being real with your entire family (and beyond) will quickly move you to the place of being an authentic man. *Being authentic is freeing.*

Chapter 5: Ingredients for Being a Good Man

What holds a man back from being real? Fear that people won't like him? Fear that people will find out he's vulnerable? Fear about not knowing who he would be if he didn't have a façade?

For the first 41 years of my life, being real scared the hell out of me. I lived behind a mirror. I was so afraid of being real, I reflected back to you what you were. If you told me you were a democrat, I was a democrat. If you told me you were a republican, I was a republican. If you liked vanilla ice cream, I liked vanilla ice cream. If you were to ask me a question about me, particularly regarding my religion, I would cleverly avoid answering. Instead, I'd turn the conversation back to you by asking you a question. I was afraid you'd find out who I was. My strategy for living behind a mirror was a survival technique I learned as a child.

One of the reasons I lived behind a mirror was the fact that both of my parents were Reform Jews. I was a Jew. I was a Jew in a community of gentiles. For the first seven years of my life I lived at the top of a hill at the end of a cul-de-sac. There was only one way in and one way out. Every time anyone in my family went down the street, if my neighbor, Todd, was outside in his yard, he'd throw up his arm, raise his middle finger, and yell at the top of his lungs, "Jew, Jew, fucking Jew!"

When my family moved about one mile away, I was seven years old. The neighbors were much more welcoming, and I had friends up and down the street. High school, however, became challenging when supposed friends of mine started calling me, "Kike" and "Jew boy."

Outside of my family, I was the only Jew I knew in my community until I was a junior in high school. That's when Jean, another Jew, moved into the neighborhood. Everyone thought we would get married. We didn't, but we were great friends.

Chapter 5: Ingredients for Being a Good Man

Through the influence of several Christian families in my neighborhood, I started to question my religious beliefs. I eventually converted to Christianity and accepted Jesus, a fellow Jew, as my Lord and Savior. I took Him at His word when He said He was the Son of God. Before my conversion, I had to search my soul to make sure I was accepting Christ for all of the right reasons. I didn't want to hide my Judaism in a Christian package just to blend in and avoid ridicule, hate, and shame.

Now you know why I lived behind a mirror; why I couldn't be real; why I was afraid to be real. A couple of trusted friends who valued my Jewish history more than I did, helped me to come out from behind my mirror and own my Judaism. By that time in my life, I felt safe in acknowledging my Jewishness and I was strong enough to stand up for myself. I felt safe enough and strong enough to be real. Being real was freeing. Being real required much less energy than hiding secrets. I felt a load lift from my shoulders.

People notice authenticity. Being real seems rare in our society. When I see an authentic man, he stands out from the crowd. I'm drawn to him because I want to know his story. I want to know how he arrived at being authentic. What impact does his being real have on his family? His co-workers? His health?

Men seem to die too young. According to statistics, men are dying early and before women. *Why do men die early? Why are men drawn to drugs and alcohol to numb their pain instead of reaching out to a counseling professional or support group?* Could it be that men rarely process their emotions? If that's the case, then all of their fear, sadness, loneliness, and grief are stuffed down into their body. Maybe "men want to be men," which means being tough and, therefore, never going to the doctor for a check-up or when something appears to be wrong. Could it be that

Chapter 5: Ingredients for Being a Good Man

it takes a lot more energy to keep things inside than share them with others for fear of appearing weak? I don't know for sure, but I would like to propose the idea that if more men were able to be real (reveal who they truly are and seek help to overcome their struggles), we would see less men dying from heart attacks, drug overdoses, alcohol poisoning, and suicide.

In her October 31, 2019 article called "Life Expectancy for American Men Drops for a Third Year," Aimee Picchi for CBS News MoneyWatch stated, "Life expectancy for U.S. men slipped for a third straight year, according to new data from the National Center for Health Statistics. The average male lifespan stood at 76.1 years in 2017, a four-month decline since 2014. Drug overdose rates for men are almost twice as high as a decade ago."

What if being real allowed you to live longer? Would it be worth it to change? It is not healthy to hold your true self in bondage. I encourage you, no matter the consequences, to share your truth. Of course, not everyone will love it, but that is their problem, not yours. Trust me, those who love you will adjust, and their respect for you will grow in the long run. If you truly want to take a step toward being real, it might be in your best interest to consult with a religious leader or counseling professional to work through the process in advance.

Now that you have a little more insight into the ingredients that make a good man, let's continue to look at what it takes to be a good man from a spiritual perspective. In the next chapter, you will discover what God teaches about mature masculinity.

Chapter 5 Exercise

Is there a church or community center in your area with a men's program?	
Yes	No

If you answered yes to the above question, are you willing to explore the idea of getting connected with other men?	
Yes	No

Why or why not?

Ingredient #1: Being Responsible

How do you *feel* when you take on more responsibility?

Chapter 5 Exercise

How do you *benefit* when you take on more responsibility?

How does your spouse/partner benefit when you take on more responsibility?

How do your children benefit when you take on more responsibility?

Chapter 5 Exercise

Ingredient #2: Being Respectful	
Do you realize your words and behaviors can tear others down or lift them up?	
Yes	No
Do you listen to others when they are upset, or do you make it all about you?	
Yes	No
Do you pay attention to the tone you use when you speak?	
Yes	No
Do you pay attention to your body language when you communicate?	
Yes	No
Do you respect your spouse/partner as much as (or more than) you respect a stranger?	
Yes	No
Do you respect your children as much as (or more than) you respect a stranger's or neighbor's child?	
Yes	No
Ingredient #3: Being Reliable	
Do you expect reliability from others, especially those who you are closest to?	
Yes	No

Chapter 5 Exercise

How do you feel when you can't rely on someone?		
Can your spouse/partner rely on you?		
Yes		No
Can your children rely on you?		
Yes		No
Ask your spouse/partner if they can rely on you. If they say they cannot, are you willing to change your behavior?		
Yes		No
Ask your children if they can rely on you. If they say they cannot, are you willing to change your behavior?		
Yes		No

Ingredient #4: Being Real

Have you ever met a man who was real, truly authentic? What characteristics or behaviors were apparent to you?

Chapter 5 Exercise

How would you feel if you were authentic all the time?	
Do you understand how it takes more energy to hide your true self than it does to be real?	
Yes	No
If being real allowed you to live longer, would it be worth it?	
Yes	No
Are you ready to start being real all the time?	
Yes	No

HonorOurSons.com

Chapter 6

What Makes a Man?

"Every man must decide whether he will walk in the light of creative altruism or in the darkness of destructive selfishness."
~ Martin Luther King, Jr.

What makes a man may be difficult to answer, but it's important to answer. Your son is watching you. Not only is he watching, but he is also learning and modeling your behaviors. When you fully understand what makes a man and live as a man, your son will have a path to follow towards his manhood because you led the way. As a result of your efforts, your son will have increased his odds of ultimately living an honorable life. Think of the struggles you have had in life. What if your son doesn't have to struggle in the same way, or struggles less, simply because you are his role model of healthy masculinity?

Beyond the physicality, a man is made up of his values, morals, behaviors, character, emotions, passions, and much more. Society often reflects that a man is tough, strong, in charge, blameless, and entitled because he's "THE MAN." Therefore, he has the right to hold power over women and children, destroy and abuse people and things when he gets angry, do what he wants when he wants, make sexual innuendos towards women, and go out at night whenever and with whomever; but this kind of person is not a real man. This behavior is that of an out-of-control, impulsive, self-serving little boy in a man's body. These kinds of behaviors may be hiding deep unfulfilled needs or emotional and psychological childhood wounds.

It seems an important aspect of a man is one who values himself, exercises self-control, and is open to correction for the sake of maturing. In what areas of life do you struggle most with self-control? *Is it money? Sexual impurity? Laziness? Anger? Not being a servant? Not taking responsibility?* Let's look at some of the cool insights God has regarding each of those issues.

If you are not a man of faith, that's fine. You don't have to believe what I believe. If you decide to skip the text, you certainly can. Or, you may want to read the text from the Bible to see what you can learn, what you want to take with you to apply to your life, and what you want to leave behind.

The following Bible verses come from a portion of the Bible study I facilitated with each one of my sons on their respective initiation and blessing weekend. This study was organized by the Pastor of the church I was attending at the time. Not being a Bible scholar, I was pleasantly surprised at how much instruction was in the Bible about how to behave as a man. Take your time in reading each selection so you can extract the critical components you want to keep. I will conclude this chapter with a Psalm that wasn't in the original Bible study for my sons, but has a number of juicy bits of instruction for men (and women).

Self-Control

Proverbs 15:32

*Those who disregard discipline despise themselves,
but the one who heeds correction gains understanding.*

Chapter 6: What Makes a Man?

As a boy matures into a man, his focus moves from self-serving to serving others. At the heart of mature masculinity is a sense of servant responsibility to lead, and leadership requires self-discipline. Put another way, Gary Smalley and John Trent in their book *The Hidden Value of a Man* say, "The degree of self-control you have in life is in direct proportion to the degree of acceptance you have for yourself. If you don't value yourself, you won't pull in the reins on actions and attitudes that will affect you for the worst."

Money

1 Timothy 6:10
For the love of money is a root of all kinds of evil. Some people, eager for money, have wandered from the faith and pierced themselves with many griefs.

Hebrews 13:5
Keep your lives free from the love of money and be content with what you have, because God has said, "Never will I leave you; never will I forsake you."

2 Corinthians 9:6-8
Remember this: Whoever sows sparingly will also reap sparingly, and whoever sows generously will also reap generously. Each man should give what he has decided in his heart to give, not reluctantly or under compulsion, for God loves a cheerful giver.

Worship God; don't worship money. Be content with what you have and never worry about money because God will not abandon you. Give generously and give with a happy heart.

Chapter 6: What Makes a Man?

Sexual Impurity

Proverbs 5:3-10

For the lips of an adulteress drip honey, and her speech is smoother than oil; but in the end she is bitter as gall, sharp as a double-edged sword. Her feet go down to death; her steps lead straight to the grave. She gives no thought to the way of life; her paths are crooked, but she knows it not. Now then, my sons, listen to me; do not turn aside from what I say. Keep to a path far from her, do not go near the door of her house, lest you give your best strength to others and your years to one who is cruel, lest strangers feast on your wealth and your toil enrich another man's house.

Proverbs 5:18-23

May your fountain be blessed, and may you rejoice in the wife of your youth. A loving doe, a graceful deer —may her breasts satisfy you always, may you ever be captivated by her love. Why be captivated, my son, by an adulteress? Why embrace the bosom of another man's wife? For a man's ways are in full view of the Lord, and he examines all his paths. The evil deeds of a wicked man ensnare him; the cords of his sin hold him fast. He will die for lack of discipline, led astray by his own great folly.

In these passages, King Solomon is warning us to steer far from any person who tries to lure us to them for less than honorable reasons and who might be lost themselves. Don't fall to temptation, and don't be the tempter or temptress. Stay clear of adultery. Make noble decisions and defend your boundaries that result in your sexual purity and your commitment to intimacy with only your spouse.

Chapter 6: What Makes a Man?

Laziness

2 Timothy 2:15

Do your best to present yourself to God as one approved, a worker who does not need to be ashamed and who correctly handles the word of truth.

Paul, a follower of Christ, teaches us to work in such a way that God will approve of our efforts. Don't get distracted. Don't be lazy. Stay focused. Always do your best, be truthful, and be open to constructive feedback.

Anger

Ephesians 4:26-32

In your anger, do not sin. Do not let the sun go down while you are still angry, and do not give the devil a foothold. Anyone who has been stealing must steal no longer but must work, doing something useful with their own hands, that they may have something to share with those in need. Do not let any unwholesome talk come out of your mouth, but only what is helpful for building others up according to their needs, that it may benefit those who listen. Get rid of all bitterness, rage and anger, brawling, and slander, along with every form of malice. Be kind and compassionate to one another, forgiving each other, just as Christ God forgave you.

If you use anger as a defense mechanism or have uncontrolled anger, I recommend professional counseling. Anger management is critical to your loved ones' well-being, and yours. If you have unresolved anger towards someone—your parents, siblings, co-workers, neighbors, spouse, or child(ren)—do all you can to work through the conflict. Unresolved conflict will eventually undermine or poison your relationships.

Chapter 6: What Makes a Man?

Be willing to share your feelings appropriately, listen without interrupting, and put away your ego. A man who can exhibit these behaviors is honorable, strong, and powerful. He's a man of deep character, earning respect for his courage, forthrightness, and humility.

This type of admiration can also be achieved with your vocabulary. I'm often surprised by the cuss words that come out of men's mouths. Mature men can get their point across without using foul language. A man who becomes keenly aware of his speech might become shocked at his immature communication style. A noble, authentic, and honest man communicates to lift others up.

Being a Servant

Luke 22:26

The greatest among you should be like the youngest, and the one who rules like the one who serves.

This passage is about servant leadership, encouraging humility. You may be the head of the household or the boss at work, but your title shouldn't set you apart from the young—the inexperienced. I've applied this strategy at work by never asking my co-workers to do something I wouldn't do. The same applies at home. I have the role of husband and father, but my responsibility is to serve my family.

Taking Responsibility

Genesis 3:9

*But the L*ORD *God called to the man, "Where are you?"*

Chapter 6: What Makes a Man?

There is a lot of insight found in this passage. In summary, God put Adam to work in the Garden of Eden and commanded, "You are free to eat from any tree in the garden, but you must not eat from the tree of knowledge of good and evil, for when you eat from it, you will certainly die."

When Eve joined Adam, she was tempted by the serpent to eat the fruit that *God instructed Adam not to eat*. As you probably know, Eve ate the fruit. Now you might say Eve is to blame for the fall of man because she went against God and ate the fruit. However, Adam is to blame. Adam was right there with Eve, and he didn't step up—he didn't protect Eve, nor himself, as they both ate the fruit.

Instantly Adam's and Eve's eyes opened, causing them to become aware of good and evil. While covering their nakedness with fig leaves, they heard God walking in the garden, so they hid in shame. Even though God knew where Adam was hiding, He called to Adam, "Where are you?" Adam answered, "I heard you in the garden, and I was afraid because I was naked; so I hid." God replied, "Who told you that you are naked? Have you eaten from the tree I commanded you not to eat from?" Instantly, Adam blamed Eve for giving him the fruit to eat. Adam told God, "The woman you put here with me—she gave me some fruit from the tree, and I ate it."

Adam did what many men do—we blame someone else rather than take responsibility. As men, we must step up to do all we can to take responsibility, own our decisions, own our mistakes, and admit the truth, all while protecting our family. Real men don't throw others under the bus to protect themselves.

I struggled to be a mature man for decades. When I converted from Judaism to Christianity, my conversion didn't instantly solve all of my problems. If anything, my belief in Christ increased my awareness of who I was, how much I needed to change, and how much I needed a Savior in Jesus Christ. Unfortunately, the changes I needed to make took years to come to fruition. Since I'm imperfect and own the fact that I'm a sinner, I'm separated from God. However, since Christ died for my sins on the cross, my relationship with God is restored by His grace through faith in Jesus Christ. *How cool is that!?*

Now here is the juicy Bible selection I promised you at the opening of this chapter. This passage is from the book of Psalms and is Psalm 15, a psalm of David taken from the New International Version (NIV) of the Bible.

> *Lord, who may dwell in your sacred tent? Who may live on your holy mountain? The one whose walk is blameless, who does what is righteous, who speaks the truth from their heart; whose tongue utters no slander, who does no wrong to a neighbor, and casts no slur on others; who despises a vile person but honors those who fear the Lord; who keeps an oath even when it hurts, and does not change their mind; who lends money to the poor without interest; who does not accept a bribe against the innocent. Whoever does these things will never be shaken.*

This passage above begins by asking, who can live with God? The answer is, I can and so can you. All we must do is:

- behave appropriately so we can't be blamed for anything.
- act according to the divine or moral law.
- speak the truth.
- don't defame someone else.
- don't wrong our neighbors.

Chapter 6: What Makes a Man?

- don't hurt people with our words.
- detest a bad person but honor those who fear the Lord.
- keep our promises even when it's difficult to do.
- lend money to the poor without charging them interest.
- don't accept bribes in return for condemning the innocent.

These do's and don'ts are a tall order to fill. Now here's the best part. If we fail in our efforts to be this type of human being, and we will fail from time-to-time, we can be forgiven by admitting our failures, our sins, and asking God to forgive us in the name of Jesus. Jesus died on the cross for our sins so we can be seen sin-free when we die and meet God face-to-face. Just imagine the kind of man you would be if you focused on being the kind of man described in Psalm 15.

Who do you look up to? Who is your role model for your maturing process? Is there a man in your life who exemplifies true masculinity, a healthy masculinity? Is this man willing to be available if you need a sounding board? I hope you have such a person in mind. If not, I encourage you to be on the lookout for such a man. While you're looking for the right man, what can you do in the meantime to jump start your progress towards mature masculinity? Are you willing to consider following Psalm 15? Are you willing to research mature masculinity online and read a book or two about the subject? Could you host a weekly small group of men who have similar interest in growing as a man?

When you find your role model, I know he'd be honored if you were to ask him if he'd be willing to build a friendship with you for the sake of your growth. You never know, but his willingness to mentor you may add value to his life, too.

HonorOurSons.com

Chapter 6 Exercise

Are you willing to give money to those in need?	
Yes	No
If you answered yes to the above question, begin today by using the spaces below to plan your charitable donations.	
Dollar goal to donate each month:	$
Recipient of donation:	
Start date:	
Are you willing to go without, so others don't?	
Yes	No
If you answered yes to the above question, begin today by using the space below to set your start date as to when you will begin looking for ways you can go without so others don't.	
Start Date:	
Do you struggle with infidelity or lust?	
Yes	No

Chapter 6 Exercise

If you answered yes to the previous question and you want to stop this behavior, write the date when you will make every effort to control your infidelity and lust.
Start Date:
Do you succumb to the tempter or temptress?

Yes	No

If you answered yes to the above question and you want to stop this behavior, write the date when you will make every effort to refuse temptation.
Start Date:
Do you indulge in pornographic material?

Yes	No

If you answered yes to the above question and you want to stop this behavior, write the date when you will make every effort to stop indulging in porn.
Start Date:
Do you struggle with anger?

Yes	No

If you answered yes to the above question and you want to stop this behavior, write the date when you will make every effort to control your anger.
Start Date:

Chapter 6 Exercise

Do others tell you that you are any of the following? If yes, circle all that apply.	
Mean	Controlling
Scary	Intimidating
Demanding	Heartless
Unreasonable	Closeminded
Do others tell you that you need counseling?	
Yes	No
Do you think it is time to understand the source of your negative emotions or unhealthy behavior and seek counseling?	
Yes	No
If others are encouraging you to seek counseling and you are willing to begin counseling, use the space provided below to begin the process of securing a counselor.	
Date I will call a counselor:	
Name of counselor I can contact:	
Phone # of counselor:	
Could you be serving your family better?	
Yes	No

Chapter 6 Exercise

In what ways could you be serving your family better?		
1.		
2.		
3.		
4.		
5.		
Do you often think of yourself as being better than others?		
Yes		No
If you answered yes to the question above, why do you feel you are better than others?		
Could you stand to be more humble?		
Yes		No

Chapter 6 Exercise

If you believe you should be more humble and are willing to begin working to make it happen, use the space provided below to write your start date.
Start Date:
Do you protect your family in all realms of life?

Yes	No

If there are areas in which you do not protect your family, what are they?
Are you willing to begin working towards protecting your family in these areas?

Yes	No

In the appropriate areas, are you willing to share (with your spouse) in the leadership of your household?

Yes	No

If you answered yes to the above question, what will you begin doing immediately to share in leadership?

Chapter 6 Exercise

Do you blame others when things go wrong?	
Yes	No
Do you take responsibility for your actions?	
Yes	No
Who do you look up to? List at least 3 names.	
Name:	
Name:	
Name:	
Who, in your life, exemplifies mature and healthy masculinity?	
Name:	
Name:	
Name:	
Are you willing to contact at least one of the men you named above for the sake of building a mentoring relationship?	
Yes	No

Chapter 7: How Do Women Want to Be Treated?

Chapter 7
How Do Women Want to Be Treated?

"If you find it in your heart to care for somebody else,
you will have succeeded."

~ Maya Angelou

I can already hear you. "Henry, why do you have a chapter titled *How Do Women Want to Be Treated?* in a book about honoring our sons?" Great question! Here's the answer. Before I could honor my sons, I had to be an honorable man. To be that man, I had to understand what it means to be a man, what a man looks like in his words and actions, how to be present and engaged, and how to treat women, particularly my wife. Only then was I prepared to focus on honoring my sons.

I grew up with an unhealthy interest in women. This unhealthy interest was because my introduction to the female body occurred way too early. My mom and dad never knew this, but a babysitter of mine crossed physical boundaries with me as early as five years old. As one of my therapists told me, "Your sexual window opened way too soon." She was 100% correct. This abuse, which went on for several years, set me up for poor decision-making regarding boundaries with women.

Yes, some men might slap me on the back and congratulate me on the success of my sexual conquests, and even say to me,

Chapter 7: How Do Women Want to Be Treated?

"You da man!" but those guys aren't men. In fact, I wasn't a man. I was a teenage boy in a man's body, and I would hesitate to call these "back-slapping men" my friends. Men who were my true friends would want the best for me. If my true friends had known what was going on, they would have talked to me about my behaviors and held me accountable for my decisions. A man would have lovingly confronted me in hopes of changing my destructive path to a life-giving path. This approach may not always work, but a man—a true friend—must try.

Part of the craziness of my poor decision making was that I knew right from wrong. When I was acting out, the wrong felt good, at least for a short while, because it numbed the emptiness, shame, guilt, insecurities, and fear I felt. However, I'd always feel emptier, more shameful, guilty, insecure, and fearful after the fact. For years, I justified my wrongdoing by blaming my babysitter. *It was her fault. She did this to me. I was an innocent victim.* Or I would blame my mom and dad for not protecting me when I was young.

How long can I claim to be an innocent victim? At what point do I start taking responsibility for my life, for my actions? When do I decide to confess my sins to God, ask for forgiveness, make amends where I can, and trust God, through Christ, to carry my guilt and shame?

As parents, our children watch every move we make. Learning what your wife wants will pour life into your relationship with her while modeling for your son how a man should treat the woman he loves. Showing your son how to appropriately treat women is one of the most important acts you can do as a father. If we are arrogant, macho men, workaholics, adulterers, video game/computer/TV addicts, and jerk-ball husbands to our wives, our sons will see our behavior and be at risk of

Chapter 7: How Do Women Want to Be Treated?

mimicking our behaviors. Likewise, if we are sad sacks, weak, passive, non-committal, distracted, and lack direction, our sons will mirror those traits, too. To that end, we must earn the right to lead our sons into manhood. Before we can do that, we must have our act together; however, we don't have to be perfect. Being imperfect and aware of our imperfections helps to honor our sons into manhood because it is the imperfections that help create humility—a much-needed attribute when it comes to being vulnerable with our sons.

Women are strong and smart, and deserve our honor and respect. Unfortunately, the world, and often the work-world, don't always see them as such. Our home is a different world, or at least it should be. Women should be able to come home, feel safe, relax, let their hair down, and be respected. Some men understand women and behave appropriately. Yet some men disrespect their wives in a variety of ways.

There are men who come home from work thinking their workday is done, so they hop on their bike and go for a ride before dinner, instead of helping their wife and children. Other men grab a beer and head off to their man cave until dinner. In short, men can isolate themselves from the real needs of their family. Meanwhile, the mother (who is working in or out of the home) is preparing dinner, managing the children, helping with homework, and taking the dog out for a walk.

On the other hand, some men may help with the housework and children, yet belittle their wives for one thing or another. These are the same men who take the stress caused by their work, and their inadequacies and insecurities, out on their wives, children, and family pets. (They tend to act out through verbal, physical, and/or emotional abuse.)

Chapter 7: How Do Women Want to Be Treated?

Home should be a place of refuge where your wife knows you are there to lead and to follow, depending on the circumstance. For example, if your wife is cooking dinner, ask how you can help. If she doesn't need help with the cooking, you can help by setting the table, clearing the dishes, loading the dishwasher, scrubbing the pots and pans, or assisting with the children. When it comes time to eat, sit down at the dinner table with an attitude of gratitude. If you complain about your wife's cooking, surely your kids will follow suit. Instead, thank your wife for the great meal. Then, when dinner is over, take the lead and help clean up as a family. Teach your son to be pro-active and to work as a team, knowing when to lead and when to follow. Remember, he is watching you.

If you're not a man of faith, you don't have to say grace before your meal, of course. Instead, you could lead a conversation about how grateful you are for the time, effort, and skill your wife invested in making a great meal. On the days when you do the cooking, I'm sure you'd appreciate positive affirmations, as well.

If you are a man of faith, beginning your meal with a short prayer is a great time to express your gratitude for the meal in front of you. Leading a prayer can be intimidating for men. I have found it's not what is spoken during the prayer that makes grace intimidating, rather it's a false belief we will be perceived as dumb because we don't know what to say. Men might also be reluctant to lead a prayer for fear of appearing weak because he's making himself vulnerable by showing his spiritual side. Quite the opposite is true. Praying before a meal is a sign of humility, strength, and leadership, and God will be pleased with whatever you say, as will your family. Also, prayer is powerful in building your family's foundation and strengthening

Chapter 7: How Do Women Want to Be Treated?

the bonds between each of you. Men of all faiths pray. Giving thanks before a meal can be simple.

> "Dear God,
> Thank you for my wife and her hard work in preparing this food. Thank you for our family and this time we can spend together. Amen."

If you're not a man of faith, your message of gratitude might sound like this:

> "Before we begin our meal, I'd like to take a moment to express my gratitude to my wife for putting together a great meal and for my son who helped in setting the table. Let's enjoy!"

It's my hope you're the type of man who is keenly aware of his wife's needs and pro-actively satisfies those needs. If your wife is often frustrated, short-tempered, angry, closed off, or unwilling to be intimate with you, have you ever wondered why? If so, you should ask her. Maybe Ms. Angelou has the answer you need below.

> *"Never make someone a priority when all you are to them is an option."*
> *~ Maya Angelou*

Ouch! Why should your wife make you a priority if she is only an option for you? Take a moment to ask your wife if she feels like your #1 priority.

Encourage and support your wife, listen to her, speak with a loving tone, anticipate her wants and needs, love her with all your heart, share your heart with her, surprise her with flowers or an overnight trip for just the two of you, and pray with her. You may never be able to do everything perfectly to hit a grand

Chapter 7: How Do Women Want to Be Treated?

slam home run, but when you put forth the effort consistently, you'll get darn close. As a result, I'd bet your wife would respond much differently to your romantic overtures.

The truth is, you and I will never be perfect, and that's okay. When mishaps occur, talk to your wife about the situation at hand. Let her know you recognize the areas you need to improve and then listen as she shares her perspective. How you think you are doing may not be how she thinks you are doing. Therefore, take responsibility to make sure you're both on the same page.

Have you asked your wife how she wants you to treat her? If not, now may be as good a time as any. Make it your goal to have a great conversation about this topic. Be open. Be a great listener. (Taking notes may help.) Don't get defensive. Hearing what your wife has to say is the first step towards change, but the act of listening to her comes with a WARNING. Here is the warning… if you don't follow through on what she says or on what the two of you agree upon, then you have just made your situation worse. From her perspective, it becomes "Business as usual." "He doesn't care about me." "He's full of crap; typical." "He was just listening for the sake of listening and never intended on taking me seriously." "Why do I stay with this loser?"

To drive home the point about how disappointed your wife might feel if you don't follow through, let's look at this example from the man's perspective. Let's say you want more physical intimacy in your relationship with your wife. Have you told your wife what you want? If you haven't, then don't expect her to read your mind. Be sure to let her know. For the sake of this example, let's say you did tell her what you want regarding your physical/sexual needs. You even asked her if she could commit

Chapter 7: How Do Women Want to Be Treated?

to satisfying those needs, and she said, "Yes, I promise." You feel great, now, knowing you won't live your life sexually frustrated. BUT... she never follows through. What are your thoughts now? "Business as usual." "She doesn't care about me." "She's full of crap; typical." "She was just going along with me yet never intended on following through on her commitment." "Why do I stay with her?"

Can you see the similarities between the two scenarios? When your wife shares her wants, needs, and desires, it doesn't mean you've done your part. It doesn't stop there. You don't have to fulfill every one of her wants, needs, and desires, but you must *do* something. You must take action just like you'd want her to take action if the roles were reversed. As a husband, it is your responsibility to serve your wife.

I realize there are many options available for how a man and a woman can carry out their respective roles in the family. I have often witnessed women carrying the bulk of the responsibility and decision-making regarding matters involving the family and the home. Sometimes this approach is out of necessity because the man is in the military and deployed overseas or travels a great deal for work. There can be any number of legitimate reasons why the woman must be in charge. However, the case can be made that some women are tired of making all the decisions and being responsible simply because her husband has chosen to hide behind his passivity and is unwilling to partner with his wife.

The question, "How do women want to be treated?" is an important question. It becomes even more important when rephrased to, "How does your wife or partner want to be treated?" Maybe you and your wife agreed that your marriage is a partnership. If that's the case, I hope the two of you have

Chapter 7: How Do Women Want to Be Treated?

talked about your respective roles, duties, and tasks, agreed upon them, and carry them out to the joy and satisfaction of you both.

There are many phases of life for men and women, and how they function as a couple. There are also traditional and non-traditional roles for men and women, and how they work together. The point is to engage with your wife or partner in a conversation about where she is in her life and how she wants to be treated. She might reciprocate by asking you, "How do you want to be treated?" Once the two of you have had this discussion, it is incumbent upon each of you to act on your verbal agreement.

Being a man, a husband, and a father is hard work, selfless work, and often thankless work. The same can be said for being a woman, a wife, and a mother. Don't be a husband and a father for the glory, because it may not come. Be in a close relationship with your wife and children because it's the right thing to do, it is what men do, and it's what your wife, children, and community need from you. You can do this! Your son is watching you.

Chapter 7 Exercise

Do you have friends who "pat you on the back" when you do immoral acts or speak ill towards women or your wife?	
Yes	No
If you answered yes to the above question, are you ready to make better decisions by not engaging in immoral acts and speaking ill towards women and your wife?	
Yes	No
When you see how your friends act against women or their wives, are you ready to speak up to tell them they shouldn't act that way?	
Yes	No
Knowing your son watches every move you make and mimics your behaviors and words, are you proud of how you modeled for him how to treat women?	
Yes	No
What is your typical behavior when you get home from work? Do you isolate or help your family?	

Chapter 7 Exercise

Do you provide an environment for your wife that is safe, relaxing, and respectful?	
Yes	No
If you answered yes to the above question, are you willing to double-check your answer with your wife to see if she agrees with you?	
Yes	No
In what ways can you better respect your wife?	
How can you begin to help your wife more at home?	
Do you pray with your family?	
Yes	No
If you don't pray with your family, why not?	

Chapter 7 Exercise

If you don't pray with your family, are you willing to commit to trying?	
Yes	No
Do you allow your kids to disrespect your wife?	
Yes	No
If you answered yes to the above question, what do you get out of allowing disrespect to take place? (Saying, "I get nothing out of it" is not a valid response.)	
If you allow your kids to disrespect your wife, are you willing to put an end to it?	
Yes	No
Have you ever asked your wife how she wants to be treated?	
Yes	No
If you have asked your wife how she wants to be treated, have you followed through by taking action on what she said?	
Yes	No
If you have not asked your wife how she wants to be treated, are you willing to ask her now?	
Yes	No

Chapter 7 Exercise

Does your wife withhold intimacy from you?	
Yes	No
If your wife withholds intimacy from you, can you find a reason in your behavior as to why she withholds it?	
Yes	No
If you answered no to the above question, are you willing to engage your wife in conversation so you can find out why she withholds intimacy from you?	
Yes	No
If you answered yes, indicating you can find a reason in your behavior as to why your wife withholds intimacy from you, are you willing to change your behavior?	
Yes	No
As you ask your wife about her desires and how she wants to be treated, write one response in each box. Then, circle the ones you can act on immediately and act on them. Be sure to add to the list the things you are confident your wife would love for you to do, but she didn't think to tell you.	

Chapter 7 Exercise

HonorOurSons.com

Chapter 8
Ingredients for Being a Good Father

*"To be what you've never been,
you must do what you've never done."*

~ *Unknown*

Shortly after my wife and I were seated for dinner at a local restaurant, a young family sat down within my line of vision and very close to our table. The mother and her two sons (approximately ten and twelve years old) headed to the restroom, leaving the dad at the table. When the oldest son returned, his dad didn't look up from his phone. A few minutes later, Mom came back and asked the whereabouts of her other son. When she realized he was still in the restroom, she turned around and headed back to get him. When Mom left, Dad leaned forward and glared at his son, asking him in an angry tone, "Why didn't you wait for him?" I didn't hear the son's response, but he lowered his head, hiding his eyes under his ball cap. Dad, obviously displeased and still angry, shot a few more comments at his son, then sat back in apparent disgust, shook his head, and reunited with his phone. Within seconds after Dad stopped verbally beating his son, Mom and the other son returned.

Now that you have read the story above, keep in mind my assessment of what was going through everyone's thoughts and hearts is merely my judgment. In addition, there are always two sides to every story, and sometimes three sides. I only tell that story to shed light on fatherhood. Before I matured as a father, I reacted the same way this dad did when my sons made similar errors in judgment. What I wasn't aware of at the time is how much damage I was doing to my sons when my frustrations weren't expressed appropriately. Just like I judged this young boy's spirit to be broken by his dad's words and glaring stare, I know there were times when I broke the spirits of my sons. Even though it's been over thirty years since my sons were little boys, I can still recall four (and I know there were more) such occasions as if they were yesterday. Remembering these four events brings up feelings of sadness, shame, and regret. How I wish I had reacted differently to my sons' decisions and behaviors.

Similar to the previous lists of ingredients for being a good man and husband, the list below is not exhaustive. Likewise, there can be overlap in all three lists because defining what it means to be an upstanding man, husband, and father is just as complex as identifying the individual components. Being intentional, transparent, and loving, for example, can be ingredients for a man, husband, father, employee, boss, friend, and more. With age providing me 20/20 hindsight, decades of experience, and tidbits of wisdom, let me share the basic ingredients for being a good dad.

Ingredient #1: Love and Empathy
Love is the most important ingredient. In 1 Corinthians 13, the Bible states that between faith, hope, and love, "the greatest of these is love." Boys need physical affection from their dad as well as their mom.

Chapter 8: Ingredients for Being a Good Father

Combine the love for your son with a dose of empathy. Look at the world through your son's eyes. If you're 6'0" tall and he's only 3'6", you can look mighty intimidating to him. As an experiment, lower yourself to his height, then imagine looking up at someone who is 6'0". The view is vastly different from down there. Add in your deep voice, and it's easy to see why it's important for you to earn your son's trust. If you can, keep your son's view of the world foremost in your mind—especially when you're disciplining him. This perspective, that of putting yourself in your son's shoes, may motivate you to change the way in which you administer discipline. For example, consider physically lowering yourself so you can be eye level with him before you discipline him appropriately. Think of it this way, the last thing you want is for your son to be sitting in a therapist's office when he's older, working through the fear he had for you or trying to understand why you never said, "I love you."

My sons are in their mid-thirties, and I text them a heart emoji or "I love you!" from time-to-time. When I'm doing a video chat with them or visiting in person, we always part ways saying, "I love you." Even more, I still hug and kiss them on the cheek or forehead.

I remember kissing my dad on occasion. The one kiss I'll never forget is the one I gave my dad on Sunday, February 10, 1985. I had flown into town a few days earlier to visit my dad in the hospital. He had suffered a heart attack on January 30th, and the doctors weren't sure he would make it. Over the next several days, my dad seemed to be improving, so we decided it was okay for me to return home. As I said goodbye to him, I leaned over the edge of his hospital bed, lifted up his oxygen mask, and kissed him on the lips. We said, "I love you" to one

Chapter 8: Ingredients for Being a Good Father

another, and I left. Two days later, I had to fly back into town because he died of a massive heart attack on Tuesday, February 12, 1985, at the age of 66.

The importance of the love between a father and son can't be overstated. This love relationship is to be cherished and protected. If your dad didn't tell you he loved you and didn't give you hugs and kisses when you were growing up, don't let that be your excuse for not expressing your love to your son. I encourage you to break the generational chain by loving on your son. You won't regret it, and neither will he. In fact, his future wife and children will also be grateful for the love you have shown him. Think about it. You have the ability to impact generations to come. Whether the impact will be positive or not-so-positive is based on the choices you make today.

One final note about love. A lot of dads say, "My son knows I love him." When I ask, "How does he know?" Overwhelmingly, the response has something to do with how much the dad *does* for his son, not what the dad *says* to his son or how the dad physically expresses love for his son. For instance, dads will say, "I go to work every day and bring home a paycheck, so my son can eat and have a roof over his head." "I pick him up and drop him off at school and basketball practice." "I attend every one of his football games. That's how he knows I love him." When dads are asked, "How does your son know you love him?" It would be a game-changer if every dad said, "I tell him verbally that I love him and I express my love physically by giving him a hug, a pat on the back, a fist bump, or a high five."

Dads, there is no "expiration date" on loving your son. In other words, if you're an older dad and your son is a grown man, but you've never told him you love him or how proud

Chapter 8: Ingredients for Being a Good Father

you are of him, the "good through" date is until your last breath. Step up, summon your courage, soften your heart, be vulnerable, and say to your son, "I love you, and I'm proud of you." Expressing your love for your son by doing things for him isn't enough. That's the easy way. Anybody can *do things* for other people. The more challenging but meaningful way, is to verbalize your love. The three words, *I love you*, can shift your relationship with your son from good to beyond great. Don't take those words for granted.

Sons, no matter your age, if you've always wanted to hear "I love you" from your dad, the "start date" is today and the expiration date is the date of your last breath. Start today by telling your dad, "I love you." Oftentimes, sons must jump-start this process by modeling it for their dad. If it feels awkward, don't give up. The more you tell him, the easier it will become for you. Be consistent. Over time, your dad will hopefully reciprocate by verbally expressing his love for you. If this strategy is too abrupt, take your dad aside for a chat the next time the two of you are together. Maybe the conversation starts by asking your dad what his relationship was like with *his* dad around the expression of love. Something like, "Dad, how do you know that Grandpa loves you?" Then bring the conversation around to telling your dad what you want. Let him know what it will mean to you if he tells you that he loves you, verbally. Every son wants to hear "I love you" from his dad. I just wish every dad knew this nugget of wisdom and acted on it.

Ingredient #2: Tenderness and Strength

Tenderness embodies affection, kindness, gentleness, and showing concern. Tenderness in a woman is often assumed and associated with the feminine gender. Tenderness in a man is rarely seen and often associated with being unmanly because it

Chapter 8: Ingredients for Being a Good Father

is easily lost in society's portrayal of the stereotypical man; so go against the grain. Be gentle and affectionate with your son. At the same time, be strong. Strength isn't a reference to the size of your biceps or how much you can bench press. This kind of strength refers to your character, inner strength, feeling grounded, and poised to stand the dark storms of difficulty. Tenderness and strength may seem like polar opposites, but using them together can produce a confident, powerful sense of security and love for your son.

What do tenderness and strength look like? When my sons were of high school age, I was in the kitchen when Jon (one of my sons) walked in. I immediately stopped what I was doing, walked right up to him, looked him in the eyes, and said, "Stop! Put your hands to your sides. Look me in the eyes." I placed my hand on his heart and said, "I love you!" He told me he loved me, as well. After we hugged, we went about our business. Three or four days later, I was busy with some task when Jon walked in, told me to stop what I was doing and look him in the eyes. He placed his hand on my heart and said, "I love you!" Through tears, I told him I loved him, too. We hugged, then went about our business. I was deeply touched.

Other examples of tenderness and strength could include:

- Giving a warm hug to your son
- Praying on your knees with him
- Getting his undivided attention and telling him how much you love him and how much he means to you
- Offering words of affirmation
- Pro-actively helping him with his homework without getting frustrated
- Inviting him to go for a walk or run with you

Chapter 8: Ingredients for Being a Good Father

- Taking time to gently massage his back or feet when you put him to bed
- Asking him for his opinion

Ingredient #3: Self-Control

Good fathers have to apply self-control in many different circumstances. I'll offer up two areas as examples. The first is giving your son room to grow, and the second is expressing emotions appropriately, particularly anger.

Many parents want to "save" their children. Meaning, rather than have their child make a mistake, parents will take over, direct, redirect, or go out of their way to ensure their child doesn't crash and burn. If parents overly protect their children by keeping them from making mistakes, how will they learn to stand on their own? How will a child learn how to fix mistakes if they get no experience in doing so?

I'm not saying what my wife and I did was right or wrong, or the best or worst in this regard. But here is what seemed to work for us. Our philosophy was: It's better for our sons to make mistakes while they are of elementary school age than middle school age. Just the same, it's better for them to make mistakes during their pre-teens than their teenage years. Again, it's better for them to make mistakes during their teenage years than college age. One last time, it's better for our sons to make mistakes during their college years than as grown men in the adult world. Mistakes at the lower levels can be easier to fix and your son can learn valuable lessons. So please utilize self-control and allow your sons to *learn the hard way* when necessary, but stay close so you can offer support as needed.

When it comes to emotions, how skilled are you at expressing them appropriately? Do you "lose it" or do you maintain self-

Chapter 8: Ingredients for Being a Good Father

control? While crying may be difficult for some men to express, it doesn't usually carry the destructive nature of anger. Dr. James Dobson said, "Feelings are neither right nor wrong. It's what you do with them that causes the problems."

Anger can be a mask or smokescreen for other feelings, but it seems to be the first and easiest emotion to express—the go-to emotion for men, and some women. I'm going out on a limb here when I say 100% of the anger I've seen in myself and other men is not the real emotion being felt. Anger is a reaction, a defense mechanism that protects more sensitive feelings, which may be more difficult to express. Behind the anger is often fear or sadness, or even guilt. As a result, depending on the circumstance, I've trained myself to express my anger with words like, "I'm angry, but more than that, I'm disappointed; and here's why..." "I'm angry, but more than that, I'm sad, and here's why..." "I'm angry, but more than that, I'm afraid, and here's why..."

When I express my anger in those ways, I'm not yelling, tossing up my hands, storming out of the room, punching someone or something, throwing someone or something, destroying property, scaring people, or adding in any drama. I express my anger with intensity, "I'm angry," but I'm not yelling or acting out physically. Once I get past my anger and identify the feeling(s) behind it, I'm in a much better place to explain what triggered my anger in the first place and to express my true feelings.

There are great articles on the web about healthy ways of expressing emotions and tips on managing anger. I encourage you to do your homework.

Ingredient #4: Patience
Patience is in the same family as Ingredient #3: Self-Control.

Chapter 8: Ingredients for Being a Good Father

Being able to wait when the first impulse is to respond, is a gift for some and a learned skill for others. I wish I could say patience was one of my greatest strengths when my sons were small, but I can't; mine is a learned skill. In the first 12½ years of my sons' lives, I know I was impatient; and how I expressed my impatience wouldn't win me any awards. What's worse than my impatience was my tone and word choice. Truth-be-told, I struggle with impatience today, but not nearly at the same level as in past times. Now, when I'm out of line, I'm quick to apologize. However, an apology doesn't justify poor choices. Remaining patient or becoming impatient is a choice, and how we express patience or impatience is also a choice.

Good choices can be made before any damage is done. As a result of my impatience, I have hurt many people, particularly my sons. My words and nasty tones have scared my sons, broken their spirit, and diminished their self-worth. Think of five to twelve-year-old boys and how tenderhearted they can be, along with their limited understanding of life. At those tender ages, I expected my sons to understand what was making me impatient; but they weren't capable of doing that yet. It was completely unfair of me to think otherwise. Patience is much easier to achieve when we set realistic expectations for ourselves and don't put expectations on others.

I wish I had better understood how long it would take to grow an infant son into a young boy, a boy into a teenager, and a teenager into a man. Knowing that it takes almost two decades, I needed to be patient to accomplish this critical task. *Rome wasn't built in one day, and neither is a son.*

Ingredient #5: Teach
Many dads are already good teachers. We teach our sons to walk, talk, ride a bike, fly a kite, swim, fish, hunt, cut the grass,

Chapter 8: Ingredients for Being a Good Father

take out the trash, wash the car, shovel snow, rake leaves, and much more. But when your son is of age, will you teach him about his body? Will you teach him what to expect as he grows into his teenage and young adult years? Will you teach your son the progression he will encounter over the next fifty years from teen boy to young adult to middle-aged man to a senior citizen? Will you discuss topics such as masturbation, lust, pornography, alcohol, drugs, and smoking (to name a few)? Will you explain to your son that he'll have hair growing out of his ears and a forest of hair growing from his nose at some point in his life? Will you teach your son about God, Jesus, the Holy Spirit, faith, how to pray, and your belief system?

How I wish I could have been a great teacher when I was raising my sons. By sharing this next story with you, you'll not only see how I blew a perfectly good opportunity to teach my son, but you'll get a sense of how I matured and became a more intentional dad.

At the age of nine, one of my sons got his first pubic hair. Excitedly, I yelled to my wife to come and see. Both of us hovered over our son as he laid in bed. I was glowing with pride and bubbling over with enthusiasm, unaware of the consequences my behavior was having on him. *What did my son do?* He covered his pubic area with his hands. I noticed it, but that move didn't stop me from saying how cute the hair was and other insensitive remarks. I can only assume my son felt embarrassed and humiliated over something he didn't understand.

There, right before me, was a wonderful opportunity to start teaching my son about masculinity when he was nine years old, and I blew it. If I could have a do-over, I would have honored him by explaining what pubic hair was and that it's one of the many changes he'll experience on his journey into manhood. I

Chapter 8: Ingredients for Being a Good Father

would have then taken a few more minutes to explain some of the other changes he and his body would be going through. I would have encouraged him to watch for these changes with anticipation and a sense of excitement. But I didn't.

Three years later, immediately following my men's training weekend, I took my son aside and asked if he remembered the interaction with the pubic hair. His face flushed. He reluctantly nodded and said he did. It was three years later, and he still remembered that horribly embarrassing moment, and I felt ashamed. I apologized to him for my behavior, asked for forgiveness, and explained I was wrong to humiliate him. Kindly and fortunately, he forgave me, and I promised him and myself, I would not let something like that ever happen again.

A couple of years later, I was once again presented with an opportunity to humiliate or honor my sons. It came when it was time for me to teach them how to shave. As you might imagine, my old self would not have recognized the significance of the moment—the rite of passage. I likely would have lined my sons up in a row, made jokes about their baby-faces, and told them to shave—if I would have even done that much.

This time, I chose to honor my sons individually. I called the first one into the master bathroom and told him it was time he learned how to shave. I told him it was such an honor for me, as his dad, to take this time to recognize his growth into manhood. I explained to him that growing hair on our face is one aspect that sets us apart from women, and we have the choice to shave or not to shave. I also told him not every father has this opportunity or takes advantage of the opportunity to honor his son in this way, marking his path to becoming a man.

I explained to my son that I would show him how I shave my

Chapter 8: Ingredients for Being a Good Father

face, and then he can take a turn shaving his face. I then began to shave my face and narrated as I went, being sure to include any necessary cautionary tips while he watched. When I was finished shaving, I gave my son his own can of shaving cream, a new razor with extra blades, and some after-shave lotion. I then watched as he performed his first shave, and I reiterated the importance of having this special time together. I then repeated this process with each one of my sons.

When I reflect on that day, I recall their behavior and measure the impact of my efforts. While I was demonstrating how to shave by shaving my face, I distinctly remember the intensity of how my sons observed me in the mirror, trying to memorize each step of the process and each stroke I made with my razor. When it was their turn, I saw that same intensity in their eyes as they applied the shaving cream and then carefully shaved around their jawline and under their nose.

Years later, I asked one of my sons if he remembered when I taught him how to shave. When he said he did, I asked what he felt at that time. He replied, "A little embarrassed, but proud."

Bingo! I had hit the bullseye. While I would have liked him not to have been embarrassed, it was obvious to me he felt far more pride than embarrassment. This sense of pride is exactly what I wanted him to get from this experience. I wanted my sons to be proud that they were growing into men.

The key to being a great teacher is the style in which you teach. Don't expect to receive an A+ in teaching if you teach your son through sarcasm, shaming, teasing, or off-color jokes. It is important to teach your son with your eyes on the goal. If your goal is to give your son every opportunity to succeed, you must be the absolute best teacher you can be. You must teach with

Chapter 8: Ingredients for Being a Good Father

a certain level of gravitas and intention.

Your ability to create a safe space for you and your son to talk about intimate topics is critical to your success as a teacher. Maybe you take your son fishing, on a long walk, or sit around a campfire to create this safe space. Wherever you create this safe environment, make sure it's just the two of you and that you reassure him your conversations will be confidential. When you address your son, your words should always be honoring and supportive. You can never judge his questions as *stupid*. Every question is important, as is every answer. Maintain your composure when your son asks you questions that he thinks are serious, but you judge as ridiculous or stupid. Your response to his questions can determine the level of trust your son has for you now and in the future.

Your tone, eye contact, and ability to maintain your son's dignity is crucial. If you feel awkward or scared to talk about a topic, I encourage you to step into your awkwardness or fear. Don't back away. Once you step into the conversation, most, if not all, of the awkwardness and fear will dissipate. If you don't know an answer, tell your son, "I don't know, but I'll find out." Or "I don't know. Let's look the answer up together."

My approach was to talk more often with my sons about the topics I found to be most awkward or scary for me. The more I talked about these difficult topics, the better discussions my sons and I had, and the faster the awkwardness and fear disappeared. I came to understand that certain topics were awkward or scary for me based on the experiences I had and the feelings I associated with those experiences when I was a teenage boy.

The bonus you and your son will receive from your efforts in teaching him is that you will become your son's "go-to-guy"—

Chapter 8: Ingredients for Being a Good Father

his most trusted resource for honest information. He will see you as a safe man to come to for all his questions about any topic. Just think how this kind of mentoring will positively impact his life, your relationship with him now, and your relationship with him once he starts to build a family of his own.

Ingredient #6: Foresight
As you just learned, being your son's trusted go-to-guy will lay the foundation for future relations he has with you. Therefore, always be thinking a step or two ahead of your son. What are the next three events coming up in his life? *Is he graduating from elementary school to middle school; middle school to high school; high school to college? Is he getting married? Is acne getting ready to rear its ugly head? Is he almost ready to shave? Is the pitch of his voice about to drop? Is his body gearing up for an insatiable appetite? How soon is he going to need deodorant? Is he about to be faced with a big decision?* Once the next three events are identified, you then must decide how and when you're going to honor him with a mini rite of passage for each.

Before I give you the story of how I used foresight to grow my sons, I want you to know that what I did might appear contradictory to what I said in Ingredient #3: Self-control—specifically relating to allowing my sons to make mistakes. However, in my defense, in the following case, I wasn't focused on my sons making a mistake because the outcome would be good for them in either case. Instead, I was focused on teaching them how to stand up for themselves and face conflict head-on. Here's the story.

My sons' primary sport was soccer. When they started playing club soccer during their elementary school years, I was their coach, learning the sport right along with them. By the time they reached middle school, I was on the outer edge of my ability to teach them anything new. It was time for them to go

Chapter 8: Ingredients for Being a Good Father

to the next level. They ended up joining a more competitive team, so I went from coach to spectator. This select team had two coaches. One coach had the responsibility of teaching the boys skills and strategy. The other coach, whom I'll call Mason, handled the administrative responsibilities.

After playing on the select team for one year or so, my sons came to me and said they wanted to quit. I told them they certainly had the right to quit, but they would have to tell Mason. One of my sons told me they were hoping *I* would tell Mason. I responded that I understood what they were hoping for, but it was their responsibility to do it since they're the ones who wanted to quit.

I then started thinking about how I could use this moment to grow my sons. I came up with a two-point strategy. First, I told my sons I would teach them how to approach Mason and what they might say. We discussed approaching Mason with good eye contact and clear reasons for their decision to quit. Second, I called Mason. I told him what my sons wanted to do, but, more importantly, I needed his help. I told him I was trying to teach my sons how to stand up for themselves and approach difficult conversations, especially with someone in authority. I asked if he would listen to my sons' request with interest, acknowledge and thank them for their courage to talk to him, and respect them as young men. Beyond that, I told Mason to respond anyway he wanted and to keep our conversation confidential. Mason was fully onboard.

At the next practice, my sons were prepared to speak to Mason. When practice ended, my three sons walked up to Mason (I was standing off to the side). Two of my sons hung back a little and physically nudged Jordan to the front as if pushing a lamb to the slaughter. Jordan looked up at Mason and respectfully asked if the three of them could speak with him. Mason stopped what he was doing, gave them his full attention, asked what they had on their minds, and listened intently. Jordan explained what they wanted to do and why, to which Mason reacted perfectly. He thanked them for coming to him and expressed how mature it was to do so. He then gave them a few reasons why he thought they shouldn't quit but left it up to them to decide.

Jordan turned around to face his brothers, and they huddled for a minute. When they were done, Jordan turned to face Mason and said they would stay on the team. Mason expressed joy in their decision and shook each of their hands, thanking them for the discussion. (Wow!) This interaction between my sons and the coach was powerful. I was grateful to Mason and extremely proud of my sons for displaying bravery.

Ingredient #7: Perspective
Maintaining a healthy perspective can help you weather any difficulties you may encounter while raising your son. I learned, albeit late, to see the growth of my sons in terms of phases. They won't always be in diapers and need a bottle every two hours. They won't always be small children asking, "Why?" They won't always be teenagers who *know it all*. Once I gained that perspective, I was encouraged and knew I could finish the marathon one phase at a time. Now, I encourage you to enjoy each phase and be patient because the one they're currently in won't last forever.

Over many generations, and even today, there are few rites of passage honoring our children's transition into adulthood. The Jews have Bar/Bat Mitzvahs, the Catholics have Confirmations to reflect a child coming into an age of religious maturity, and some Native American cultures have vision quests. But what

Chapter 8: Ingredients for Being a Good Father

about the rest of the young male population?

According to Custodial Mothers and Fathers and Their Child Support 2017, a report released by the United States Census Bureau, "over one-quarter of all children under twenty-one years of age have one of their parents living outside of their household." These children are being raised by a single parent, most commonly their mother. How do boys grow into healthy, responsible men when there is no male role model in the home? For families with two parents, what are the fathers doing to honor their son's growth and transition into manhood?

The following chapters will show you what I did for my sons in order to mark their transition from boyhood to manhood. It's my hope you will find a way to celebrate *your* son's transition into manhood. As with the first part of this book, take what you need and leave the rest behind. But first, there are some questions for you to answer on the following pages.

HonorOurSons.com

Chapter 8 Exercise

To the best of your knowledge, have you ever broken your son's spirit?	
Yes	No

If you answered no to the above question, would you be willing to ask your son if you have ever broken his spirit? Of course, you may need to explain what you mean by *breaking his spirit,* so he can answer you honestly after you create a safe space for him to do so.	
Yes	No

Ingredient #1: Love & Empathy

Does your son know you love him?	
Yes	No

If you answered the last question yes, how does he know you love him?

Chapter 8 Exercise

Are you willing to ask your son if he knows you love him—more importantly, if he *feels* your love for him?	
Yes	No
Do you verbally tell your son you love him?	
Yes	No
If you answered the last question no, why not?	
If you do not regularly say, "I love you" to your son, are you willing to begin doing so starting today?	
Yes	
When was the last time you told your dad you love him?	
Approximate Time Frame:	
If you don't already, will you commit to telling your dad you love him on a daily basis?	
Yes	No
Ingredient #2: Tenderness & Strength	
How do you view tender men?	

Do you consider yourself to be tender?	
Yes	No
What are three acts you can commit to doing to display tenderness?	
1.	
2.	
3.	
Do you consider yourself to be a man of strength?	
Yes	No
What are three acts you can commit to doing to display appropriate strength?	
1.	
2.	
3.	
Ingredient #3: Self-Control	
Do you allow your son to *learn the hard way* so he can naturally mature?	
Yes	No
If you answered the last question no, do you now see the value in allowing him to *learn the hard way*?	
Yes	No

Can you commit to allowing your son to *learn the hard way* in most, if not all, situations?	
Yes	No

Does your wife allow your son to *learn the hard way*?	
Yes	No

If you answered no to the above question, are you committed to discussing this approach with your wife?	
Yes	No

Do you use self-control to allow your son to speak for himself?	
Yes	No

Will you use self-control to monitor your sideline behaviors and words when your son is playing sports or after seeing your son perform with the band, etc.?	
Yes	No

Ingredient #4: Patience

Do you consider yourself a patient or impatient man?	
Patient	Impatient

Have your words and tone ever cut into the heart and spirit of your son?	
Yes	No

Chapter 8 Exercise

Describe your typical tone and words used when you grow impatient.
What are some situations that cause you to be impatient?
What are three actions you can take to practice patience?
1.
2.
3.
Do you have any regrets for past situations when you were impatient with your son?

Yes	No

If you answered the last question yes, are you willing to apologize and strive to do better?

Yes	No

Chapter 8 Exercise

Ingredient #5: Teacher

List three safe spaces you can create for you and your son to have private conversations.

1.

2.

3.

Will you talk to your son about uncomfortable topics for the betterment of your son's future, no matter how uncomfortable they make you feel?

| Yes | No |

If you answered the last question yes, great! Appendix B is a checklist of topics that I encourage you to talk to your son about throughout his life.

Ingredient #6: Foresight

Are you the go-to-guy for your son?

| Yes | No |

If you answered no to the last question, what can you do to change this outcome?

Chapter 8 Exercise

What are the next three events coming up in your son's life that are worthy of mini rites of passage?	Write beside each event what the mini rite of passage might look like.

HonorOurSons.com

HonorOurSons.com

PART 3:
Ready to Initiate & Bless

HonorOurSons.com

Chapter 9: Rite of Passage & Ceremony

Chapter 9
Rite of Passage & Ceremony

"To be a man, a boy must see a man."
~ J.R. Moehringer

We are a few chapters away from diving into how I created and executed the initiation and blessing ceremony (later referred to as ceremony) for my sons' rites of passage (later referred to as rites). However, before we get there, it's important for you to understand what a rite of passage is, its significance, and examine a few other considerations.

Merriam-Webster defines a rite of passage as "a ritual, event, or experience that marks or constitutes a major milestone or change in a person's life." Rites of passage come in every size, shape, color, and degree of difficulty. Unless a particular rite is governed by cultural norms, religious rules, or institutional traditions, it can be as creative as your imagination. Familiar rites include baptisms, confirmations, earning a driver's license, graduations, marriage, and going through a first real job interview. Examples of more challenging rites include bar/bat mitzvahs, funerals, fraternity/sorority initiations, and military boot camp. Overall, a rite of passage sends a strong message that something uniquely important is taking place.

There are ignoble and noble rites. Ignoble rites hurt people and result in feelings of shame, regret, guilt, and humiliation. In extreme cases, they can lead to death. One example of ignoble rites involves some college fraternity initiations. So-called "big brothers" in college fraternities who haze their pledges as part of their initiation process are anything but fraternal. Unfortunately, many fraternities are the exact opposite of what brotherhood, friendship, and mutual support are all about, and their initiation rites are often immoral, illegal, and dangerous.

Another example of an ignoble rite is the scandal involving the Boy Scouts of America (BSA). Over 92,000 claims of sexual abuse were filed against the BSA. On November 16, 2020, Attorney Andrew Van Arsdale stated on CNN, "Based on what we are hearing from survivors, sexual abuse was a rite of passage in troops across the country, similar to other tasks where children had to perform certain duties to earn their coveted merit badges." The BSA's mission is to "prepare young people to make ethical and moral choices over their lifetimes…" Unfortunately, the BSA leadership has failed miserably. Lives have been devastated.

Noble ceremonies and rites for your son should result in positive outcomes such as feelings of empowerment, joy, belonging, and high self-worth, to name a few. Depending on the ceremony's content, your son may also gain a greater understanding of his life's purpose, eagerly take on more responsibility, become more focused, and experience new insights. A rite doesn't guarantee immediate changes in your son. Some changes may be immediate, while others take more time. Long-lasting, effective change takes time because new insights and behaviors need to be practiced until they are seamlessly integrated into daily habits. The rite, however, jump-starts the change process. It plants healthy seeds in your son's mind, heart, and character. These seeds may be a vision of mature masculinity, personal integrity, physical boundaries, authenticity, a sense of community with other men, and more. It's up to

Chapter 9: Rite of Passage & Ceremony

your son, you, and your son's support circle to care for and nourish these seeds so they take root, strengthen, and grow.

Importance of a Rite of Passage
For one minute, put yourself in your son's shoes. Imagine how you would feel if your dad had made an effort to honor you in a ceremony that marked your transition into manhood. *Would you feel grounded, honored, significant, blessed, humbled, encouraged, excited, and strengthened down to your core? Would you be deeply moved and motivated to become a man with noble characteristics and values?*

A rite of passage can be one of the most meaningful ceremonies your son will ever experience. His rite should lay a solid foundation on which your son can stand as he continues to mature, and it should instill a strong sense of everything good about being a man. I can almost guarantee that you and your son will be changed when you have concluded the ceremony and rite. Your son will see himself differently, in large part, because you will see him differently and treat him as a man who is one giant step closer to mature masculinity.

Building your son into a man is an admirable goal. Boys can be built into thoughtful, self-assured men, and the process can start with you and your son. Your family, community, and city will also benefit when your son becomes more responsible, mature, authentic, honest, kind, empathetic, strong in character, and outward focused. A rite of passage is important because it marks a significant event in your son's life. Overall, this life-changing ceremony acknowledges your son as he crosses the bridge from boyhood to manhood.

Is There a Perfect Age for a Rite of Passage?
I can't say there is a perfect age. The more traditional rites of passage (bar/bat mitzvahs, graduations, baptisms, confirmations

Chapter 9: Rite of Passage & Ceremony

and others), occur at specified ages. Non-traditional rites can take place anytime but should coincide with other variables you deem important. For example, the ceremony during my sons' rites took place when they were fifteen. I thought they were too young at thirteen and not yet mature enough to process all the emotional, intellectual, and spiritual information they were going to receive. When they reached fifteen, it was clear they could take in, process, and comprehend all the benefits the ceremony and rite offered them.

You will be the best person to decide when to implement your son's ceremony and rite because you'll know when he is best equipped to grasp the lessons he will be taught.

Environmental Ebb and Flow of the Rite of Passage
The ceremony that occurs during a rite (and the days and hours leading up to the initiation and blessing weekend) must engage your son at an emotional level. Develop your son's initiation weekend with a keen sense of what you want him to feel and when you want him to feel it—manage the ebb and flow of the environment you intentionally create.

For example, in the week leading up to my son's weekend, his mood was upbeat. He was excited to pack the items on his list and start the adventure with me, his dad. Friday night, as we headed out after dark, his mood changed. He appeared a little less excited because he's now more concerned; fear had crept in. When we arrived at the mountain, it was pitch black; so, he felt even more fear but was reassured because I was with him. When we arrived at the campsite, he became more upbeat because he recognized familiar camping objects used on our family trips. On Saturday, his mood was upbeat because it was just him and me doing things together. In the evening, his mood shifted back towards fear when he learned he had to spend the night alone on the mountain. On Sunday morning, his mood was exuberant because he survived the night.

If you decide to initiate and bless your son into manhood, no matter the method, event, day(s) of the week, or strategy you decide to use to honor him, be sure he's emotionally engaged. Lastly, be sure the ceremony and rite for your son is noble and the level of difficulty is age-appropriate.

Mini Rites of Passage
We're all busy, and it was no different when my sons were teenagers. Much had happened in their lives in such a short timeframe. To hit a few highlights, during their elementary years, they learned how to give someone good eye contact and a good handshake. During their teen years, they reached puberty, discovered deodorant, learned to shave, earned a driver's license, dated girls, and graduated high school and college. Since I couldn't take the time to implement a full-blown rite of passage ceremony for each of these events, I had to find an efficient solution to celebrate these milestones with my sons without diminishing their significance.

When the time came to honor my sons for achieving a particular milestone, I would perform a mini rite of passage by trying to stop the chaos of our day, or at least slow it down. For example, when one of my sons happened to be walking past me in the house, I would stop him to ask if I could talk to him for a few minutes. Then, with good eye contact and a slow, intentional tone, I would tell him, "I'm very proud of you. You now have your temporary driver's license. This achievement is one more step towards manhood for you. You're now responsible for the safety of yourself and others. There are insurance, maintenance, and fuel costs that must be paid and hours of practice to complete in order to qualify for your permanent

Chapter 9: Rite of Passage & Ceremony

license. Congratulations, and let me know if you have any questions or concerns!" I'd finish by shaking his hand and hugging him. Then, off we'd go, back to whatever we were doing. By stopping my son, slowing my speech, and speaking with a more serious tone, my son knew this moment was different than our everyday interactions.

The mini rites of passage are noble ceremonies that my sons walked away from incrementally changed. When performing a mini rite, the components that should be considered include the appropriate expression of your feelings, tone of voice, choice of words, good eye contact, a solid handshake, and a hug. The message and mood are all upbeat. My goals for mini rites are to honor my sons, do so in a matter of minutes, mark the moment in his life when something significant has occurred, and word it in such a way that he can't help but walk away feeling proud, energized, and loved.

Key Take-Aways

- The initiation and blessing *weekend* is the "umbrella" term used to describe everything that takes place over the course of the weekend from beginning to end.
- I initiated my sons over a weekend. You can choose any day(s) of the week that works best for you and your son.
- The initiation and blessing *ceremony* is the program you create to honor your son.
- The rite of passage is the highlight of the initiation and blessing ceremony and marks the moment in time when your son transformed into a man in the eyes of his parents.

Chapter 9: Rite of Passage & Ceremony

- Create a noble initiation and blessing weekend that:
  - Produces positive outcomes and feelings of empowerment, joy, belonging, and self-worth.
  - Helps your son gain a greater understanding of what it means to be a man.
  - Helps to crystalize a vision for your son and his purpose in life.
  - Motivates your son to eagerly take on more responsibility, become more focused, and experience new insights.
- Your son's experience should instill a strong sense of everything good about being a man and lay a solid foundation for manhood.
- You (and your spouse/partner) must decide when your son is ready for his initiation and blessing ceremony and rite of passage into manhood. Nobody else knows the perfect age for him to make this transition.
- Control the ebb and flow of his emotions before, during, and after his initiation.
- Remember to utilize mini rites throughout the year, and do so with slow, intentional speech, a hug, and a handshake.

HonorOurSons.com

Chapter 9 Exercise

\multicolumn{3}{l}{What do you want your son to feel before, during, and after his rite of passage? Use the blank spaces to write other emotions you may want him to experience.}		
Excited	Healthy Fear	Anticipation
Proudness	Oneness	Joy
Honor	Excitement	Empowerment
Confident	Self-Worth	Belonging

HonorOurSons.com

Chapter 10: Building a Team

Chapter 10
Building a Team

"None of us is as smart as all of us."
~ Ken Blanchard

At this point, hopefully, you understand what a rite of passage is and why it's important. Moreover, you have gained an understanding of the initiation and blessing ceremony that occurs in conjunction with a rite of passage. This chapter explains the importance of including other men in the process of honoring your son into manhood. Of course, there are many great reasons to include other men, but I will focus on the top three.

Reason #1: Modeling
When you invite other men to work with you in honoring your son, you'll need to explain what you're doing and why you're doing it, since honoring sons with a ceremony is typically a foreign concept. After sharing your vision and deciding who will be on your team, you should end up with a group of like-minded men. These men will "get it." They will understand the significance of helping you bless your son into manhood.

As a bonus, the planning and execution phases of your son's rite of passage will model a process for your team that will hopefully set the stage for them to do for their son what you are doing for yours. Being a role model for others could be the spark needed to start a trend for the men in your sphere of influence.

Chapter 10: Building a Team

Reason #2: Synergy
Synergy, in this context, occurs when two or more men come together to share ideas, work together, and focus their efforts on achieving the same goal. As your son's dad, you will want to create and execute the best plan for initiating and blessing your son into manhood. If you act alone on this project, your ideas will be limited by your knowledge and imagination. If you choose to include like-minded men, their ideas and skills will further develop what you already have in mind for your son. Be open to their input and feedback with the understanding that you have the final say. The collective's ideas are more creative than any one man's ideas.

In Appendix C, you will see a chart to brainstorm ideas for your son's rite of passage.

Reason #3: Building Community
You might be familiar with the African proverb, "It takes a village to raise a child." That statement is absolutely true. There is much for your son to learn, and you can't possibly teach him everything. To give your son the best opportunity to develop into a mature man, inviting men to participate in your son's rite of passage builds a community your son can lean on when he hits rough patches and to share in the joy during celebrations.

You might ask, "Why do I want my son to talk to other men? I'm his dad!" First of all, your son may not feel comfortable approaching you about certain topics—especially if you are known to be impatient or lose your cool. Second, the men you choose to be in your son's support circle are all gifted differently. Having more than you for your son to pick from will give him options and a chance to work through issues from a different perspective. Third, it is safer to have your son approach men you have vetted when seeking counsel, rather than

Chapter 10: Building a Team

his peers whose perspective and understanding of life are not fully developed; and surely, you do not want him to figure out life's many challenges on his own. Fourth, I mentioned in chapter one that life is a team sport. Having trusted men "on the bench" waiting for your son to call them into his game of life for support is an incredible gift. Finally, you may not be around when your son needs you. Your son may have an issue crop up while you're out of town on business or a romantic getaway with your spouse. God forbid, maybe you pass away. Whatever the case, having a support circle whom your son can count on for help is priceless.

When you introduce your son to the right men, you will know these men understand your intentions for your son. These men will have helped you implement the ceremonial rite of passage and witnessed your son transition from boyhood to manhood. The men you involve will be like-minded when it comes to honoring your son throughout the rest of his life.

In Appendix D, you will see a chart for you to write the names of the men whom you would like to include on your team.

Another Step Further
An idea you might consider is initiating and blessing more boys than just your son. I'm sure your son has friends at school, on his sports team, or in his neighborhood who are similar in age. Talk to their dads, sharing with them what you've learned in this book. Tell them of your plans for a ceremonial rite of passage for your son to see if they are interested in participating with their sons.

Pulling together a small group of dads who want to honor their sons at the same time you honor yours can enhance the expected outcome. If this joint venture is the direction you decide

Chapter 10: Building a Team

to go, be sure to include in your agenda multiple opportunities for quality one-on-one time for each boy and his dad. Having a group of boys go through a rite of passage at the same time is great, but you don't want your son to feel like he's lost in the crowd and unnoticed by his dad.

Key Take-Aways

- Be sure to clearly explain to other men what you are doing and why you are doing it, along with how their involvement is vital to your overall success.
- Be open to your team's input and ideas. You make the final decisions.
- It is critical for your son to have a support circle of men whom you pick and trust.
- Check to see if other men in your community are interested in a group rite of passage.
- Understand that one-on-one time with your son is critical for strengthening your relationship with him.

Chapter 11

One-on-One Time

"Every father should remember that one day his son will follow his example instead of his advice."
~ *Charles Kettering*

In the previous chapter, I encouraged you to include like-minded men in the planning and execution of your son's rite of passage. As a result, your son will have a circle of support that puts different perspectives within his reach as he begins his journey into manhood and throughout the rest of his life.

I also suggested initiating several boys at once. There are positives and negatives to the group approach. You and the other dads will need to analyze the pros and cons to discover the best strategy. You don't want to sacrifice the positive impact on your son that a rite of passage tailored specifically for him can have, if the group rite isn't planned and executed well. If you plan a group initiation, be sure to schedule multiple opportunities for one-on-one father and son time. Here are three great reasons to take this approach.

Reason #1: Deepen Your Relationship with Your Son
One-on-one time will improve the relationship you have with your son, which is critical to his well-being and yours. Therefore, be sure to plan events that strengthen your relationship.

Chapter 11: One-on-One Time

Physical activities are always great ways to have fun and develop a deeper connection with your son because they create lasting memories through shared experiences. Hiking, fishing, tossing a baseball, throwing a Frisbee are some examples. Don't let your ego or competitive nature spoil the fun. Having alone time with your son gives you a chance to build him up by making an effort to reinforce and raise his self-esteem. Sincere compliments go a long way towards helping your son feel good about himself. Watch for the opportunities to present themselves. "Great toss!" "Good catch!" "Well done." "That was a great hike. You've got a nice, strong stride."

Meaningful conversations with your son are another way for you to deepen your relationship with him. In advance of your time together, make a list of topics you believe are important conversations to have with your son. Then, when you are alone with him, start discussing one of the topics from your list. Your conversations should seem natural to your son—no need to follow a script. Best practices dictate that you explain to your son, "What is said here, stays here." Creating a safe place for you and your son is paramount. If you choose to talk about masturbation, alcohol, drugs, sex, boundaries, integrity, etc., thoughtfully manage the conversation. Build into your son by educating him on the topics you discuss. Explaining life lessons in detail and defining terms for him matters in leading him to understanding. Pro-active listening is a must. If he hesitates or shies away from engaging with you, encourage him to share what he knows about the topic and his perspective on the subject matter. You must be prepared to share your own experiences, control your reactions, and never shame him. Also, be sure to thank him for trusting you. I can't overemphasize the importance of being transparent and honoring your son during this vulnerable time.

Chapter 11: One-on-One Time

In short, deepening your relationship with your son can be accomplished by building him up during physical activities and building into him through meaningful conversations. Then, once you get back home (post-initiation), be sure to schedule bonding time with your son since it is an investment that increases the value of your relationship.

Appendix B in the back of this book has a chart with suggested discussion topics for you to consider, along with spaces to write relevant topics of your own.

Reason #2: Verbally and Physically Express Your Love
Time alone with your son allows you to verbally express and emphasize the love you have for your son without the risk of embarrassment from having others around. If you already tell your son in meaningful ways that you love him, that's great. Don't stop. Tell your son how proud you are of the specific character traits he has shown and the decisions he's made. In chapter eight, I talked about Love and Empathy and expressing your love to your son. If you have never said, "I love you" to your son or never hugged him, this one-on-one time is the perfect time to start. Will it be scary or awkward? Possibly, but be transparent; tell him how you feel. If you can model transparency for your son, he will be more transparent. Don't shy away from this opportunity to express your love. You could impact generations when you express the love you have for your son through your words and hugs.

Several years ago, I was fortunate to meet an outstanding young man, Steve. We worked for the same company, but in different areas; and over time, we built a great friendship. Somewhere along the line, I started to hug Steve when we crossed paths during work, when we met for lunch, and as we went our separate ways.

Chapter 11: One-on-One Time

Over a few years, Steve and his amazing wife had two beautiful children—a girl and a boy. Steve wasn't raised with hugs from his dad, but that didn't stop him from expressing his love and support for his son through various means, including hugs. During one of our conversations, Steve told me, "I hug my son because you hugged me."

Do you think Steve's son will hug his son, who will hug his son, and so on? I believe Steve's son and every grandson and great-grandson thereafter will hug their sons. Generations will be impacted. Don't underestimate the impact of the relationship you have with your son. Keep in mind that the impact goes both ways. If you decide to build into your son and love him into manhood or choose not to, the impact will still exist, but the results will be vastly different. The choice is yours.

Reason #3: Share Your Spiritual Beliefs
Finally, one-on-one time provides you with the perfect time to share your spiritual beliefs with your son. If he already knows where you stand spiritually, that's great news. If your son doesn't know what you believe, now is a great time to share your story. You can also ask your son what his story is and what he believes.

I don't remember Dad or Mom having any substantial talks with me about God or spirituality. Every Sunday, my siblings and I attended our respective Sunday school classes at our Temple, while Mom taught Sunday school to elementary aged children. I don't know what Dad was doing during this time.

The only "deep" conversation I had about God was with Mom and it lasted all of two minutes when I was eighteen years old. We were leaving Temple and I asked her, "Who is Jesus?" She said, "He was a great teacher and philosopher." I then asked,

Chapter 11: One-on-One Time

"What about His claim to being the Son of God?" Mom said, "He was a blasphemer." I told her, "It doesn't make sense that you said He's a great teacher and philosopher, and a blasphemer. Blasphemers aren't great teachers and philosophers." She said, "He was a blasphemer." The end.

Several decades later, I may have learned why my parents didn't have conversations with me about God. As I was pursuing an Executive MBA degree at the age of 55 and working full time, I decided to ask my mother why she and Dad didn't prepare me for college. I told her I was intimidated by college when I was a senior in high school and even as a freshman in college. I went on to say that I had wished I completed my undergraduate and advanced degrees while I was in my twenties instead of my late thirties and late fifties, respectively.

So why didn't she and Dad sit down with me and teach me all they knew about college since they were both college graduates? Mom said, "We thought you knew." "Thought I knew?" I asked. "How could I know? I was a clueless seventeen-year-old with no idea about what lay ahead of me after high school graduation." Then it dawned on me. Could it be the same answer for spirituality? "We thought you knew." Relationships with girls? "We thought you knew." How to manage my personal finances? "We thought you knew." You get the point. Please don't assume your son knows anything about anything. Teach him! If you don't, at least ask him what he does know so you can determine his level of understanding about a particular topic. Then make a list of subjects and teach, teach, teach.

The conversations you have with your son around spirituality, and every subject, will serve him well. At some point in your son's life, he may be asked, "What or who do you believe in?" It would be helpful if you worked with him in crafting a response to that question. Not only will it inform the person who asked the question, but it will help to build your son's confidence, develop his belief system, and open the door for the two of you to discuss this topic in the future.

While it's my hope you believe in God, Jesus, and the Holy Spirit, I understand and respect that may not be the case. My point is for you to take advantage of this alone time with your son to discuss spirituality. If you're unsure of yourself in this regard, at least introduce the subject. Get a sense of where your son is in his spiritual life, and ask him if he'd be interested in joining you in meeting with a religious leader when you return home from his initiation. Then you can explore these deeper questions together.

If you and your son believe in God or a defined Higher Power, start a conversation that is more advanced than he's had in the past. If you have no faith, no God, and no Higher Power, you can talk about that, too. In either case, you can talk about your situation, as well as the different religions that exist and beliefs that make up the fascinating spiritual fabric of our world.

If you do believe in God and the power of prayer, you can end each one of the one-on-one times by praying together. Praying with your son is powerful. Think of what this one act would mean to your son, and eventually his son, and his son...

Key Take-Aways

- The purpose of alone time with your son is to build him up and build into him by teaching him.
- Weigh the pros and cons of a group rite of passage, then decide which one you prefer.
- Schedule some one-on-one time with your son and continue doing so after his rite of passage.

Chapter 11: One-on-One Time

- Physical activities are great ways to bond with your son as long as you keep your competitive nature in check.
- Verbally and physically express your love to your son so you can have a positive impact on future generations.
- One-on-one time allows you to discuss your spiritual beliefs with your son.
- If you believe in God or a defined Higher Power, pray with your son—it's powerful.

HonorOurSons.com

Chapter 12: The Mark of Manhood

Chapter 12

The Mark of Manhood

"No man has ever risen to the stature of spiritual manhood until he has found that it is finer to serve somebody else than it is to serve himself."
~ Woodrow Wilson

How can you tell who's a man and who is a boy in a man's body? Women can usually identify, very quickly and accurately, men who are men and men who are boys. Men, on the other hand, must rely on other data. Is a man a man by his height? Hair color or lack of hair? The character of his face? The size of his muscles? His tattoos or piercings? Does he have facial hair or a five o'clock shadow? Does he have a baby face? These external features can indicate a relative age, but they can't definitively answer the question of who is and who is not a man. Instead, the mark of a man can be seen in a variety of ways.

- The quality of the decisions he makes
- The depth of his character
- The maturity he exhibits
- The responsibility he shoulders
- The character of the friends he has
- The words he uses
- How he expresses his feelings
- His passive or pro-active nature

Chapter 12: The Mark of Manhood

- How he interacts with and serves others
- How he loves and cares for his spouse and family

In this chapter, I will use my sons' experiences to describe how the mark of manhood changed their lives and how I reacted to their transformation. While there were many positive effects that came from my sons' ceremonial journeys, I will identify two of them that really touched my heart and assured me that the weekend had a lasting impact.

The first positive effect was that my sons seemed to think differently and behave in more mature ways. Of course they had their moments of slipping back, but I could tell their weekend was a new beginning for them. My wife and I made every effort to treat them as young men and not as boys.

I looked for opportunities to give them additional responsibilities. Whatever the task, one we did together or separately, I would remind my sons that men take on more responsibility than boys. I paid attention to when my sons would ask me a question. Prior to their initiation weekend, I'd usually give them the answer when they asked me a question. Now, when they asked, I answered with, "What are your options?" "What would you do in this situation?" "What do you think is the best decision, and why?" My line of questioning had three goals.

First, I wanted to generate deeper thinking because it would help them consider the consequences of each option that lay before them. Second, allowing them to express their opinions and verbally process their thinking supported them in feeling valued and that their voices were worth being heard. Finally, answering my sons' questions with a question helped me manage the current circumstances they were facing. Due to my age and years of experience, I would often know what the best

Chapter 12: The Mark of Manhood

answer was to their question or the best solution for the problem they were facing at the time. If I thought my sons' decisions were good, I'd tell them I liked how they were thinking, and I thought their ideas sounded great. If I thought their decisions were too far off course and would result in harm or some other negative consequence, I'd ask them questions to redirect their ultimate decision. For example, I'd begin by asking, "What other choices might there be in this case?" We'd eventually end up with a more appropriate option, but I affirmed my sons by acknowledging they were the ones who thought of the final solution.

The second positive effect impacted how they viewed their high school friends and acquaintances. As a result of my sons' adventure weekends, they took a giant step forward in their maturity level. Therefore, when they went back to school the next fall, many of the boys at school were perceived as immature. I'm not saying my sons were better than the other boys because attaining superiority was never the initiations' intended outcome. I am saying my sons had their eyes opened during their summer adventure weekend, which gave them a heightened awareness of boy behavior versus man behavior. My sons were still fifteen, and having just been initiated into manhood didn't mean they were instantly mature men. The boys at their school were simply exhibiting age-appropriate behavior while my sons had a different, broader perspective. Here is an example of a decision my sons made after they had been initiated.

My sons were invited to a weekend party hosted by a high school friend. I can't recall how they got to the party (if my wife or I dropped them off or a friend drove them), but shortly after they arrived, I received a phone call to pick them up. Once in the car, they told me many people were doing stupid

Chapter 12: The Mark of Manhood

things and they wanted no part of it. They decided it was in their best interest to leave. Of course, I will never know if my sons would have made the same decision had they not been initiated into manhood. The desire for a sophomore in high school to fit in and be accepted by his peers is fairly strong, so staying at the party would have been the "cool" decision. My sons chose otherwise. Other factors may have been in play in their decision making. Being triplets, each son automatically had two initiated men with him from whom he could get advice. Maybe each son remembered his noble mission statement (which I will talk about more in a later chapter) and compared their respective mission in life to the activities taking place at the party and saw the disparity. Whatever motivated my sons to leave the party, I am convinced they made the right decision and I couldn't have been more proud.

It would be easy for me to build a list of expectations for my sons now that they have crossed the threshold into manhood. However, over the years, I've learned it's not healthy for me to have expectations for my wife, my sons, and anyone else. Holding expectations for someone other than myself often leads to disappointment. I had no expectations for my sons, who were now seen as men in the eyes of their parents.

After your son has been initiated into manhood, the mark of a man may be imperceptible in him, at least initially. Be patient. Patience and consistency will go a long way in building upon your son's maturation process. Reassure your son that you are there for him. Invite him to join you on a weekly walk or a drive in the car so you can reinforce what he learned on his adventure weekend. I've said it before and I'll keep saying it, one-on-one time with your son will give the two of you a chance to check in with one another without distractions and

Chapter 12: The Mark of Manhood

keep the lines of communication open. Over time, the mark of manhood will be evident in your son. Is the mark of manhood evident in you too?

Key Take-Aways

- The mark of a man does not lie in physique, facial features, tattoos, piercings, expensive cars, job titles, or community status.
- Ask questions to allow your son to discover for himself appropriate behaviors and solutions.
- Your son will not magically be fully mature after his rite of passage, adventure weekend. Slip backs will occur.
- It's important for men to think through the consequences of their decisions.
- Don't set expectations for your son.

HonorOurSons.com

HonorOurSons.com

PART 4:
Getting Started

HonorOurSons.com

Chapter 13

How I Began

*"You seek the heights of manhood when
you seek the depths of God."*
~ *Reverend Edwin Louis Cole*

In chapter one, I told you about my experience with the Mankind Project. Through that experience, I was inspired to teach life-changing lessons to my sons. It became clear that my top priority was to prepare my sons for manhood so they would feel secure in who they are, possess high self-esteem, understand what it means to be a man of integrity, have healthy boundaries, respect for others, and so on. I had no doubt my sons would be ready for life's challenges if they had the necessary tools readily available to them in their intellectual, emotional, and spiritual toolboxes. So the question became: How would I equip my sons with these tools, so the impact was memorable, meaningful, and life-changing?

During a meeting with my Pastor, I mentioned my desire to initiate and bless my sons while they were in their teens. I also told him that I wanted to incorporate God and Native American attributes. Incorporating Native American culture was important because there had been Native American overtones during my Mankind Project weekend. In addition, growing up, I was inspired by my friend, Michael, who is Native American.

Chapter 13: How I Began

Michael and his father taught me some of the rituals and dances of their culture—a culture that honors the traditions of their tribe, ancestors, and children's growth into mature adults.

My Pastor was very supportive and suggested I talk with Kent, a man in our church I had not yet met. Kent had some wooded property behind his house, and the Pastor thought it might be the ideal location to hold the rite of passage weekend. I didn't wait long before contacting Kent, who graciously allowed me to use the site for four consecutive weekends. One weekend was used to prepare the site and three subsequent weekends were used to initiate and bless each of my sons individually.

I had an idea of how I wanted the weekend to flow and what needed to be accomplished. The rite of passage weekends had to include one-on-one time, of course, between each of my sons and me. I wanted to include men from our church and the community to inspire them to do something similar for their sons and daughters. As my plan for the weekend began to take shape, I'd share my plans with my Pastor, who would always add a spiritual aspect to my ideas by bringing God and the Bible into the weekend as a recurring theme. One of the most important goals of the weekend was to teach my sons more about God and what the Bible had to say about being a man. I also wanted to make a significant mark on the timeline of my sons' lives when they knew they had become men in the eyes of their parents. Looking at their intimacy needs, discussing their relationships with women and other men, and creating a personal mission statement were just some of the topics that would be covered on their respective weekend.

Chapter 13 Exercise

In paragraph one of this chapter, I mentioned all the reasons I deemed it my top priority to give my sons a rite of passage. What are the reasons you want to do this rite for your son?

1.
2.
3.
4.
5.
6.
7.
8.
9.
10.

Chapter 13 Exercise

It was important for me to incorporate God and Native American culture in my sons' rites of passage. What theme(s) do you want to incorporate in your son's rite of passage?

You may not want to hold your son's rite of passage in the woods like I did. Where is the perfect location for your son's rite of passage?

Who do you want to contact first to get the ball rolling for planning your son's rite of passage?

What are some of your first ideas on how you want your son's rite of passage to flow?

1.
2.
3.
4.
5.
6.
7.
8.
9.
10.

Chapter 13 Exercise

What do you want to accomplish through your son's rite of passage?

HonorOurSons.com

HonorOurSons.com

PART 5:
Initiation & Blessing

HonorOurSons.com

Chapter 14: Preparation

Chapter 14
Preparation

"First find the man in yourself if you will inspire manliness in others."
~ Amos Bronson Alcott

Over the next few pages, I'll describe how I prepared for my sons' rites of passage weekends. Each weekend took place during the summer because I live in the mid-west and I'm not fond of being cold. More importantly, my sons weren't in school during the summer, so they weren't distracted by school and extracurricular activities.

First, I invited ten men from church to an early Saturday morning pancake breakfast at our church. I chose the number ten because I thought this would be sufficient. I would have been right if all ten men could have participated every time I needed them. As it turned out, I should have invited twenty men to account for conflicts in schedules and last-minute changes. I learned there is no perfect number of volunteers, but it is best to have too many men than not enough men.

I took the pancake breakfast approach because I love to cook pancakes, and I needed a hook—pancakes are a tasty lure. I really needed these men to attend and hear what I had to say.

Chapter 14: Preparation

It would have been much more difficult for me and less impactful for my sons without their help.

After everyone had eaten, we moved into an adjoining room. Before we entered, I asked each man to remove his shoes. I also had them remove the items from their pockets and place them in a baggie marked with their respective names. I included this step in the process for three reasons. First, I didn't want distractions from electronic devices and jingling keys and coins. Second, by removing their shoes, it implied we were entering a special kind of space far different from where breakfast was held, a sacred space; an area where men can be men, where a sense of privacy and confidentiality exists, and a safe place where we can be our true selves. Lastly, I wanted them to be mildly uncomfortable with what was taking place. It's been my experience that when emotions are involved, the senses sharpen.

We sat on chairs arranged in a circle so we could face each other as we spoke. Agreeing to confidentiality, I invited the men to be present in the moment while keeping themselves safe by remaining comfortably transparent. Each man was asked what their relationship was like with their father. Unsurprisingly, not one man had a warm and open relationship with his dad. They then shared how many children they had, how many were boys and girls, and what their relationships were like with their sons and daughters.

When it was my turn, I shared what my relationship was like with my father and confessed I wanted something different—something perceived to be better when it came to my relationship with my sons. I explained how I intended to initiate and bless my sons into manhood, and how the process would take place over three consecutive weekends—one weekend devoted exclusively to each boy. In closing, I informed the men

Chapter 14: Preparation

that the weekend was meant to mark a time in my sons' lives when they could look back to a specific moment when they made the transition from boyhood to manhood.

As for the roles these men were to play in this adventure, I needed their help with certain parts of the process. First, I needed several men to help me prepare the site. The location behind Kent's house was ideal, but it hadn't been used in a while. Clearing the leaves and branches, cleaning out and preparing the two firepits, and erecting a canopy were just some of the chores that needed to be done. Second, I needed some men to come to the site on Saturday night of each weekend. Third, I wanted my sons to build a network of men they can count on throughout life. I wanted my sons to know the men of their village. Fourth, I wanted my sons to learn from the stories these men were willing to share about their own lives. Finally, I wanted to role model for these men the concept of blessing and initiating our children into adulthood. It was my hope these men would consider honoring their sons and daughters with a similar ceremony.

Note: I intentionally invited a man who only had daughters. I thought his perspective, stories, experiences, and hopes for his girls would be valuable ingredients in this process and impactful for my sons to hear.

Nine of the ten men committed to helping me in some manner. The one who declined, when he described what his relationship was like with his father, he said, "Distant." During the next round, when I asked each man to share what their relationship was like with their son, he again said, "Distant." I may never know for sure, but the journey I was about to embark on with my sons may have hit too close to his heart. I honored his decision not to participate, and I told him so.

Chapter 14: Preparation

To guide you in planning your first meeting, view the following documents in the Appendices at the end of this book.

- **Appendix E: Breakfast Agenda for Meeting with Potential Volunteers**
  - This form details my agenda for the initial meeting with the potential volunteers.

- **Appendix F: Men's Breakfast Checklist**
  - This form served as my checklist for every item I needed to take to the initial meeting with the potential volunteers.

- **Appendix G: Needs Sheet**
  - I couldn't assume the volunteers knew what I needed, since what I was asking them to do was new to them. So I gave them a sheet of all my needs for the site preparation through the initiation and blessing weekend.

- **Appendix H: Rite of Passage Schedule**
  - This schedule outlines the daily schedule I followed on each weekend.

- **Appendix I: Information Sheet**
  - The primary purpose of this form was to obtain contact information for each volunteer and get a sense of where each man was in terms of their understanding about what I was asking them to do. I will expand on the other purposes for this form on the next page.

Chapter 14: Preparation

- **Appendix J: Letter to Volunteers**
  - This letter is a highly detailed letter I sent to the volunteers after the breakfast meeting. I intentionally made it detailed because holding additional meetings with the volunteers was impossible. (There was no good time when everyone could meet.) I also thought it was best to give more information than less. I didn't want any man saying, "I didn't know. You didn't tell me."

- **Appendix K: Roles Explained**
  - I broke the Saturday night gathering of men into five segments. Each segment outlined the responsibility each man had to carry.

The Information Sheet's (Appendix I) also served in getting them to start thinking about their roles in life as men, sons, fathers, and husbands. You'll notice a "Question of the day?" listed on the Information Sheet. The question of the day for my meeting was "What is your mission statement?" I wanted the men to write down their life's mission statement. I made this request for two reasons. First, I wanted to find out if any of them had a mission statement. Second, I wanted the men to think about their own lives and the impact they could have on my sons. Many of the men made up their mission statement sitting in that circle.

I gave you my mission statement in chapter one but will repeat it here since you now know more of my personal story. My mission, which may change one day, is: *To create a world without shame by loving, honoring, and respecting myself and others.*

Chapter 14: Preparation

In the next chapter, you will adventure with me through the activities that took place during my sons' rites of passage weekends. For the sake of efficiency, I will focus on writing about one of my son's weekend. Keep in mind, each of my sons experienced similar weekends with only a few minor adjustments tailored to what they liked.

Chapter 15
The Weekend with My Sons

"Man is never so manly as when he feels deeply, acts boldly, and expresses himself with frankness and with fervor."
~ Benjamin Disraeli

My sons didn't know any of the specifics about their special weekend. They only knew five data points. First, I would take each one of them away for a weekend over three consecutive weekends. Second, they knew we would be leaving at 9:30 p.m. on their scheduled Friday night. Third, I would be giving them a packing list on their respective Thursday night. Fourth, I would be taking them in birth order. Tyler first, Jon and then Jordan. Finally, their weekend was confidential—they had to commit to not sharing any information about their weekend with their brothers until all had completed their weekend adventure.

Note: Appendix L is the packing list I gave to each son. Appendix M is the packing list for the volunteers. Appendix N is the list of items I needed to take to the mountain when the volunteers and I prepared the campsite one week prior to the start of my sons' adventure weekends.

On each of the three weekends, I packed the same items as my son except for the disposable childhood item—an object my son owned that represented his childhood but he could live

Chapter 15: The Weekend with My Sons

without. My son was instructed to pack only the items listed, not to share the information with anyone (especially his brothers), and be prepared to leave at 9:30 on Friday night. When he asked me questions about the plans, I told him the answers would come as the weekend unfolded. My response caused his excitement to build with anticipation.

The night we left, driving in the dark, I pretended to lose my bearings. I wanted my son to start worrying—to start feeling something, anything. (As I said earlier, once emotions surface, senses are heightened.) My son began to doubt my ability to get us to where we needed to go, even though he had no clue where we were going. He began to show signs of concern, which I took as a good sign of emotional engagement—right where I wanted him.

We eventually came to Kent's driveway, but my son didn't know it was Kent's home. As we pulled into the driveway, no one appeared to be home (as planned). We headed into the woods and climbed the mountain behind Kent's house with only my son's flashlight on, purposefully keeping mine off so he would have to lead. As we climbed the hill, I whispered to him my concerns about coyotes and other wild animals. Again, emotional engagement was critical, and my concerns about wild animals would come back into play on Saturday night. I continued to allow my son to lead, knowing we would begin to see the campsite fifty yards into the woods.

Once he saw a tepee and familiar camping items halfway up the mountain, his fear subsided. He visibly relaxed, and we soon turned in for the night. The next morning, we arose at 7:30 and started a fire, munched on a light breakfast of granola and trail mix, and drank a few juice boxes. The intention was not to have a lot of food because heavy meals tend to make

Chapter 15: The Weekend with My Sons

people sleepy. I wanted us to be aware of one another, our environment, and the purpose of being on the mountain.

Following breakfast, we went for a walk to explore the area. We skipped stones on the pond and chatted openly. I told my son my goal that morning was to reach the grassy knoll that looked out over the valley below because it was the farthest and highest point from our campsite. We'd be visiting it again during the weekend, so I wanted him to be familiar with the location. As we walked, I talked to him about the importance of having a mission statement for his life.

We soon arrived at a T in the path. Since our goal was to see the grassy knoll, we needed to turn left and climb up the path rather than turn right to head down deeper into the woods. During our walk, I explained to my son that if we don't have a mission in life, any decision we make is the right one. On the contrary, when we do have a mission statement and commit it to memory, our decisions should keep us on the path towards our goal.

As we climbed to the top of the grassy knoll, our conversation continued. When I thought we had sufficiently covered the topic of creating a mission statement, we sat to observe the valley for a while. On the way back to the campsite, we stopped at the pond to skip a few more stones and continue talking.

At 10:00 a.m., we were back at our campsite, so I led a Bible study, giving credit for the content to our Pastor who created the study, "What Makes a Man?" (Appendix O is the outline for the Bible study.) During the study, my son and I took turns reading the Biblical references, using each reference as a starting point for deeper discussion. The study led to a better understanding of how God intends men to behave.

Chapter 15: The Weekend with My Sons

In addition to the Bible study, we played a game dealing with intimacy needs. First, I gave each of us a copy of the Intimacy Needs Sheet (Appendix P), something I created with my Pastor's help. We had fifteen minutes to identify our top three intimacy needs. Then we guessed what the top three needs were for each other before revealing our true needs. I asked my son to give me examples of what each one of his needs looks like so his mother and I could work on fulfilling them. For example, one of my sons picked "Appreciation" as his number one intimacy need. When I asked how I could appropriately express my appreciation for him, he told me he likes it when his efforts are noticed and encouraged.

When we finished our discussion around intimacy needs, we ate a small lunch then enjoyed the next segment of fun and adventure. I customized the fun to the interest of each son. For Tyler, we baked an upside-down pineapple cake in a Dutch oven. I tossed the Frisbee and baseball with Jordan—both a little difficult in the woods, but doable. I played chess with Jon and afforded him time to read a short book about dating. During our downtime (while the cake was baking on Tyler's weekend and Jon read his book on his weekend), I'd whittle, write in my journal, or read the Bible.

When my son and I were done with our leisure time, we talked more about his life's mission. I explained his mission statement must have a vision and an action. When he had a better understanding of the elements of a mission statement, I sent him off to the pond with his pen and notebook. I told him he could spend the time skipping stones or sitting in the chair I had placed by the pond; but while there, he needed to create his mission statement. He could then return to camp. While he was at the pond, I prayed and wrote in my journal.

Chapter 15: The Weekend with My Sons

Note: I found it fascinating that each son, albeit triplets, were so different. Tyler was at the pond for about fifteen minutes, Jordan about forty-five minutes, and Jon about ninety minutes.

When my son returned to the campsite, we discussed his mission statement. We identified the vision and the action and boiled down the language to be more concise. I never told him what to write, but I did ask questions to help him express his vision more clearly. This process allowed us to polish it and make it his unique mission statement.

The next step was to memorize his mission statement. So back to the pond he went. Upon his return, I asked him to recite his mission statement from memory. If he seemed unsure of the words or hesitated in any way, I pressed him to repeat them. I explained there are times in life when a split-second decision needs to be made. For example, should he smoke, drink alcohol, take illegal drugs, commit a crime, etc.? The mission statement needs to be recalled instantly to make good decisions when peer pressure is in play.

As the afternoon wore on, there was time to incorporate a few more lessons, but I decided not to—just hanging out was great quality time. Instead, we relaxed, prepared the fire, and talked. After dinner, we stoked the campfire and lit the lantern that hung on a nearby tree. In the woods, under a full canopy of trees, it became dark relatively quickly. So we ventured to the grassy knoll to watch the sun go down and the lights of the towns below come on. The goal was to have my son out of the campsite area by 8:00 p.m., so he didn't see the men arrive.

In preparation for the walk, I took a flashlight and a kerchief. I put the kerchief in my back pocket so my son didn't see it. As we passed the pond, we stopped to skip a few stones to

Chapter 15: The Weekend with My Sons

compete for the greatest number of skips and see who could get a stone to skip across to the other side. (My sons won on both counts.)

As we headed from the pond to the grassy knoll, I talked about the gifts I had received through many of life's losses. I explained that a loss is an opportunity to find out more about who he is, his character, and who he wants to become. I told him he could allow a loss to break him or help build him into a better man by deepening his character. At 8:45 p.m., I suggested we call it a night and head back down to camp.

Note: One of my sons became bored on the grassy knoll watching the sunset. He made it clear he wanted to head back to camp earlier than scheduled. I did two things to delay our departure. First, I told him to give me a few more minutes so I could enjoy the peace. During that time, I tried to engage him a bit more in conversation about the stars, how magnificent the world is, how small we are, and how important we are to God. As we talked, I decided he just needed to be moving around, so we got up and started walking around the knoll. (I give you this note so you can be prepared to improvise.)

Since the men from our community were at the campsite and getting ready for our arrival, I was highly aware that I was on a timetable. Therefore, I used the pond as a buffer. It was a means of adjusting the timeline by skipping stones again if we were running early or simply passing by the pond if we were running late.

After we passed the pond, I told my son it was time to blindfold him with my kerchief. I was amazed at how much each of my sons trusted me, expressing no concern or fear to what came next. When the blindfold was in place, I spun him around slowly a few times to add to the suspense, then led him back to

Chapter 15: The Weekend with My Sons

camp. As we walked, I told him he had to trust me to watch out for his safety, making sure he didn't hit any low-hanging tree limbs or step into any potholes along the trail. I also told him he would meet many men throughout his life, and he needs to find the ones he can trust versus the ones who will let him down. He needed to be on his guard and find the men with whom he could be vulnerable. I explained how men like to compete for jobs, women, cars, and money, but it is important to have a small circle of male friends with whom none of those things matter and who will bless his life and encourage him.

When we reached the camp, I led my son past the blazing campfire and into the tepee. I carefully guided him around the candlelit firepit in the center of the tepee to the seat of honor.

As I helped him onto the chair, his hand reached back to feel where he was going before finally settling in. I let him sit there for a few seconds in silence, then instructed him to take off the blindfold. After his eyes adjusted to the light inside the tepee, he was surprised to see he was part of a circle of men who were wearing masks. Most of them came with masks made from paper grocery bags, though a few had on Halloween masks.

Photo by Henry Saas

Chapter 15: The Weekend with My Sons

As my son took in his surroundings and looked at the masked men, I took this time to explain that most men he will meet will wear a mask. Some men will express how much money they have (a false confidence or arrogance), while others might try to convince him how wonderful their life is, although their marriage is falling apart, they're on the brink of bankruptcy, or they suffer from depression. Be aware of the masks men wear, but most importantly, search for the man behind the mask.

The men then removed their masks. My son spent the next few seconds sitting in silence, making eye contact with each man. Most of the men were from church, and a few were from our community. My son either knew each one personally or had seen him at church or around town.

Once my son had taken enough time to process his surroundings, I told him all he had to do was sit and listen to these men share their life's lessons in hopes he would be able to apply the lessons to his life. I also told him he could trust these men, and they would be available any time of the day or night to provide support throughout his life.

I decided to lead the group, figuring if I shared first, it would set the tone and build a level of trust within the circle. I talked about the relationship I had with my dad and the shame I felt growing up due to events that took place when I was a child. After I was done, the other men shared their stories and lessons. Some talked about their mistakes, while others talked about what they would do differently if they could have a do-over on their life. These men knew no topic was off-limits—addiction, gambling, work, alcohol, pornography, cigarettes, and drugs were all welcomed.

Chapter 15: The Weekend with My Sons

Sitting in a tepee in the woods at night with everyone sharing old wounds made it easier for each man to share. The man in attendance who only had daughters had received instructions from me to share what kind of man he was looking for to "knock on his daughter's door." Other than that, I didn't rehearse, prompt, or control this segment of the weekend.

As the men shared, I looked around in awe of the commitment these men made for my son and me. I felt blessed. One man brought a walking staff and wore a beaded necklace. Another wore a necklace and placed a bearskin on the seat of honor. These were surprises that conveyed to me they understood the significance of this weekend and their roles. Their decision to add these visuals enhanced the ambiance, boldly capturing the theme of the evening. I am forever grateful.

When the sharing concluded, I directed everyone outside to the campfire. The men stood around my son, who stood in the center with the disposable childhood item he had packed. I explained that the childhood item was a symbol of his childhood and childlike ways. When he was ready, he could throw his symbolic item into the fire as recognition to himself and others that he was becoming a man. However, I did encourage him to keep one thing from his childhood—his childlike faith in God.

When my son was ready, he tossed his childhood symbol into the fire and watched as the smoke and ashes drifted upward. Next, my son stood in front of me as I looked him in the eye and told him how proud I am of him and that I love him unconditionally for who he was, is, and will become. I then placed a red leather necklace I made around his neck to symbolize his passage into manhood. The necklace was made of a leather shoelace meant for a boot. Attached to it was a small red piece of leather tied into the shape of a small bag. In the bag were

Chapter 15: The Weekend with My Sons

small symbols made of pewter, representing important aspects of his life—a cross representing his relationship with God and a soccer ball representing his love of soccer. I also included a pinch of dirt from the mountain representing the sacred land where he was initiated. Lastly, I added two small stones symbolizing his testicles—his manhood—because when a boy goes through puberty and enters manhood, his testicles increase in size, drop lower, and changes occur in his scrotum.

The men and I laid our hands on him while I led a prayer of blessing over my son and expressed my deep gratitude for the men in his circle. When I completed the prayer, with the most serious expression I could muster, I told my son there was only one thing left to do tonight (I paused for dramatic effect), and that was… to eat! I supplied the paper plates, cups, napkins, and plasticware, and the men provided soda, chili, casseroles, and desserts. One man who was gifted in music brought his guitar in the off chance we had time to sing songs.

We spent the rest of the evening eating, celebrating, and socializing. When everyone was done eating, we took a group picture so my son could remember everyone who participated. After the picture, I told my son there was one more thing to do—finalize his journey into manhood by spending the night alone on the mountain. He seemed slightly concerned… emotional engagement at its best.

Note: This moment in the weekends is why I whispered my concern to my sons about coyotes, wolves, and other wild animals as we ascended the mountain Friday night. I wanted them to feel some degree of fear so the outcome in the morning would be one of success and survival. I also hoped they would pray for God's protection.

With the reality sinking in that he would be alone on the

Chapter 15: The Weekend with My Sons

mountain, the men and I packed up the buffet, said goodnight to my son, and headed down the mountain. At the bottom, I expressed my gratitude to the men and sent them off to a well-deserved night of sleep.

Note: My sons didn't know I was sleeping at the bottom of the mountain. As far as they knew, I went home to sleep in my bed.

Each night before I went to sleep, I wrote some of my thoughts about the day in my journal, which I'll share with you in the following chapters. I hope, by reading my journals, you will gain more insight into the weekends.

Each Sunday morning at 7:00, I would climb the mountain to rejoin my sons. When they came out of the tepee, each of them exhibited similar body language. If I had to slightly exaggerate what I saw, I'd say their chest was puffed out and they felt six-feet tall and bulletproof. Based on their body language, they seemed to feel very good about themselves in a humble way.

The scariest part of the weekend for my sons was sleeping alone on the mountain. I refer to this event as "the ordeal" because at 15½ years old, sleeping alone in unfamiliar woods is a big ordeal. When I arrived at the camp each Sunday morning, I found each son handled "the ordeal" in slightly different ways. Tyler stacked all the wooden chairs and whatever else he could find in front of the tepee door. Jon attempted to do the same as Tyler but only used one chair. Jordan was too tired to do anything and went to bed exhausted. I am happy to report all three of them survived the night. When they woke up and came out of the tepee, I told them how brave they were to spend the night alone and how happy I was they survived.

After exchanging a "Good morning," I asked them to think of a feeling and attach it to an animal that best describes what they

Chapter 15: The Weekend with My Sons

felt. In each case, they came up with an animal within a few seconds of being asked.

Tyler was happy and the most authentic I had ever seen him; he was vulnerable, joyful, and proud. As a result, he said he felt like a Joyous Elk.

Jon chose Walking Wolf (he later changed it to Wandering Wolf). The weekend seemed to slow his pace a little so he could be present, in the moment, and vigilant for the sake of absorbing everything he experienced.

Jordan chose Soaring Eagle. He was flying high and feeling extremely confident about who he was at that moment.

After the animal name had been identified, we had a hearty breakfast of cereal, yogurt, and juice. We packed up the campsite and headed down the mountain. Since it was Sunday morning, I timed our departure so we could go home, shower, and meet the rest of the family at church.

• • •

What you just read is the culmination of a whole lot of detailed planning. Your plan can be completely different than mine. Any good plan with detailed steps on how and when to execute your son's rite of passage, can lead to success.

The next section of this book is called "Reflections" and is where you will read my journal entries, hear first-hand from my sons when they were 24 years old, and read their biographical information. In the next chapter, you can scan a QR Code to watch a recorded interview between my sons and Elena Rahrig, my publisher.

HonorOurSons.com

PART 6:
Reflections

HonorOurSons.com

Chapter 16

Reflections

*"Waste no more time arguing what a
good man should be. Be one."*
~ Marcus Aurelius

In the previous chapter, you read a play-by-play of the weekend adventure I planned for my sons, including their rite of passage ceremony. The next nine chapters focus on each of my sons individually, devoting three chapters to each of them.

The first chapter for each son contains the journal entries I wrote. My entries are not particularly detailed or lengthy since I had little time to write during the weekend. The second chapter for each son is a retrospective of their initiation and blessing weekend and was written, at my request in 2008, approximately 8½ years after their initiation into manhood. In this segment, you will notice that Tyler and Jon reference this book. You might ask yourself, "How can Tyler and Jon, in 2008, reference their dad's book which was completed in 2021?" I'll just say this about that... God created the heavens, the earth, and so much more in less than one week but it has taken me years to write *Honor Our Sons*. In 2008, when I asked my sons to write a retrospective, my sons knew then that I was eventually going to write a book about their weekends, hence, the reference.

Chapter 16: Reflections

The third chapter for each son is their respective biography to give you an insight into what these fine men have accomplished since high school. Here is a test question. Will you know that my sons are men from their biographies? The correct answer is, "Probably not." You will only know if you get the chance to discover their individual characters, identify their ingredients, and observe their attributes.

Enjoy!

Taken in 2008, 8½ years after their adventure weekend.
From left to right: Tyler, Jon, and Jordan
Photo by Henry Saas

Elena Rahrig, my publisher, interviews my 37-year-old sons in February 2021.

Chapter 17
Henry's Journal About Tyler's Ceremonial Weekend

Saturday, June 19, 1999
2:17 p.m.
I'm sitting on a chair in the woods right now, watching the fire blaze in the pit. The canopy of leaves is fifty feet up from the ground. It's a beautiful Saturday, and Tyler is with me. He is on his adventure weekend. He is 15½ years old and just completed the 9th grade with straight B's. I'm very proud of his efforts. He and I both know he could be achieving better grades, but I know when I was his age, I had a tough time staying focused and studying. Tyler and I have to go on a hike right now—more later.

7:13 p.m.
The other men arrive in less than two hours. Tyler wrote his mission statement as: "To love and respect myself, others, and things I come in contact with." His #1 action step is to pray.

The fire, candles, and torches are lit. Dusk is coming. The weather is outstanding (low humidity, few to no mosquitoes).

Chapter 17: Henry's Journal About Tyler's Ceremonial Weekend

Sunday, June 20, 1999
1:03 a.m.

I'm sitting in the room above Kent's garage. Tyler is in the tepee on the mountain with God. The men have come and gone. I'm scared right now. I don't want Tyler to be alone (even with God). I want to be there with him, but I know I can't. Only six hours to go.

As I review the evening's events and my words to others, I'm not happy with myself. I wasn't perfect. However, a lot of good took place tonight. I pick at the bad or that which could have been done better.

I was so caught up in all that was going on, I forgot to take a picture of the group of men who attended Tyler's weekend. Fortunately, I was able to have one man in the picture before he and I headed down the mountain for the night, leaving Tyler in the woods.
Photo by Henry Saas

Tyler was taking a break with juice-in-a-box.
Photo by Henry Saas

Chapter 18: Tyler's Initiation & Blessing

Chapter 18
Tyler's Initiation & Blessing

*"At the center of the universe dwells the Great Spirit.
And that center is really everywhere. It is within each of us."*
~ Black Elk

My mountain name is Joyous Elk, which reflects my fervent desire to live life to the fullest by laughing and learning. My goal is to make the most of my life and do so with unyielding values and unshakeable integrity. My mission is to love and respect myself, others, and all things I come into contact with.

By this point in the book, I am certain my father has described to you how the weekend transpired. (Going to the pond to skip stones, walking in the woods, and sitting around a campfire talking man-to-man.) There is one particular event that taught me many lessons. On Saturday evening of my initiation weekend, my father had planned something unique. Blindfolded, I walked into the tepee and sat down on something hard. The eye covering I was wearing was taken off, and before me sat six masked men. At first, I was nervous, but curious. Who could these people be?

Chapter 18: Tyler's Initiation & Blessing

After a brief silence and a few words from my father, the men took off their masks and revealed their identities. These were men whom I knew and trusted. They had come up the mountain to honor me and give me, with love, the lessons of their lives. Over the next hour, they shared their perspectives on what they saw in me that made me special—made me Tyler. It's not like my parents didn't tell me these same things, but the unbiased nature of others' comments reinforced my belief that I truly had something to offer the world. We, humans, are incredibly powerful. We can dream mighty things, yet feel powerless. We can earn incredible amounts of money, yet feel empty inside. We can also take what others say about us and turn the comments into catalysts that can change our lives. These men's stories, and the sincerity with which they shared them, gave me a renewed sense of what I was on this Earth to do: *make a lasting difference.*

That night I had to sleep on the mountain by myself—as an independent man—I was scared to be alone in the tepee without a door to keep the bugs (and bears!) out. Thus, the irony is exposed. Here I am, a newly honored man, stacking coolers in front of the entrance to where I'd be sleeping. Men can be scared, right?

As I lay on the cot I set up, I realized my life was pretty darn good. I have a family who loves me, despite my many flaws. I have men who respect me for who I am and what I bring to the table. I have the "next steps" as to what I should do to grow into my manhood.

Becoming a man is not a one-time event, but a continuous inward reflection and self-improvement process, balanced by failures and successes. To me, becoming a man means:

Chapter 18: Tyler's Initiation & Blessing

- being conscious of what I say.
- being conscious of what I do.
- being conscious of how my words and actions affect others.
- treating women with respect.
- learning how to share emotions with composed candor.
- using "I" statements and assuming responsibility for my actions.
- setting healthy boundaries.
- realizing I don't have to prove anything to anyone except myself.
- being real, reflective, and revealing.
- living with intention.
- breaking through stereotypes.
- having faith that the road less traveled will lead somewhere great.

By: Tyler Saas
3/18/08

HonorOurSons.com

Chapter 19
About Tyler

After high school, Tyler went on to the Culinary Institute of America in New York, where he earned an Associate Degree in Occupational Studies with a concentration in Culinary Arts. As a trained chef, he decided to complete his Bachelor of Arts degree in Hotel, Restaurant, and Institutional Management from The Pennsylvania State University.

Immediately after receiving his bachelor's degree, Tyler enrolled in the Fisher College of Business at The Ohio State University, where he earned his MBA. He spent several years working for J.P. Morgan Chase & Co. in Columbus, Ohio and New York City before becoming employed at Deloitte & Touche in New York as a Sr. Consultant. Over five years, Tyler self-studied and earned a CPA (Certified Public Accountant), a CFA (Chartered Financial Analyst), and a CTP (Certified Treasury Professional) certification.

Tyler left Deloitte, where he had been promoted to a manager role, and went to work for a few years at Columbia University in their Treasury Department. He left Columbia and went back to work at Deloitte in their Higher Education Division, Strategy, and Operations. About five years later, he left Deloitte again and is currently working at Clemson University in South Carolina as their Associate Vice President for Budget, Financial Planning, and Analytics.

Chapter 19: About Tyler

Tyler has been a triathlete and competed in Ironman competitions. He married Darbi Roberts in December 2013. Darbi graduated from Columbia University in May 2016 with her Doctorate in Education (Ed.D). In addition, she has been an Ironman competitor and works at Southern New Hampshire University as their Associate Dean in the School of International Engagement. Tyler and Darbi live in Greenville, SC and have one child.

Chapter 20: Henry's Journal About Jon's Ceremonial Weekend

Chapter 20
Henry's Journal About Jon's Ceremonial Weekend

Saturday, June 26, 1999
2:50 p.m.
Jon and I came up the mountain last night. He is now at the pond creating his mission statement. It's hotter this weekend than it was last weekend—more humid for sure. An animal visited our site last night before we got here. It chewed a hole through a paper bag and baggie and went for the granola. It didn't get much because we showed up.

A little frog came out from under a rock that made up the ring of rocks surrounding the firepit. I told Jon to get the shovel and move the frog out of harm's way. I also said he could try to catch it since he had gloves on. (I saw Tyler do it last weekend with success.) As Jon bent down to catch it, the frog jumped and landed in the fire and died. Jon was sad. He buried the poor froggy.

I'm so proud to be the father of Jon, Jordan, and Tyler. I have tremendous joy in watching them grow, mature, and struggle.

3:37 p.m.
Jon is still not back from the pond. Whoops! I see him coming down the trail now.

Chapter 20: Henry's Journal About Jon's Ceremonial Weekend

Sunday, June 27, 1999
1:45 a.m.
I just got into bed in the room above Kent's garage. Another God-blessed evening. There was a major thunder, lightning, and rainstorm while we were in the tepee. No one got wet. To God be all of the Glory and Honor! Amen.

6:04 a.m.
A light fog covers Kent's spread. I didn't sleep very long— the room was hot and humid. I got bit up again, too. Last weekend a spider bit me multiple times on my chest and back. My thoughts this morning are centered on the awesome and mighty power of God. It is difficult for me to even begin to understand the many blessings He's given me and His ability to assemble the men in my life who are supporting my efforts in this initiation and blessing ceremony. I'm deeply moved by the gift these men have given my sons and me. I pray I have the opportunity to give back to them in the same way.

Jon is still on the mountain as I sit in my van by Kent's barn— it's beginning to rain.

Jon's mission statement is: "As a man of God, I will go to Heaven. Meanwhile, I will glorify God by helping others and having a positive impact on others' lives."

Note: In the next chapter, you may notice that Jon changed his mission statement. Mission statements are meant to be changed since we, as human beings, change and grow.

Chapter 20: Henry's Journal About Jon's Ceremonial Weekend

A group picture of the men on Jon's weekend. Jon is in the back row, and I'm in the front row.
Photo by Henry Saas

On the way home from Jon's rite of passage weekend, he held a container of chili brought to the Saturday night potluck by one of the men. Unfortunately, I had to suddenly stop, and the chili spilled soaking his pants, shoes, and floor of the car.
Photo by Henry Saas

211

HonorOurSons.com

Chapter 21: Jon's Initiation & Blessing

Chapter 21
Jon's Initiation & Blessing

"All men who feel any power of joy in battle, know what it is like when the wolf rises in the heart."
~ *Colonel Theodore Roosevelt*

At the time of this writing, it's been nearly ten years since my initiation and blessing ceremony. It was a significant marker in my life and continues to impact me today.

I will briefly touch on the setup because my father has gone into greater detail with you about it. All I will say at this point is, the weekend was shrouded in secrecy. My brother had gone the previous weekend, and all I knew of it was that he and my father had gone away for the weekend. I wasn't sure where they had gone. I remember being uneasy as the weekend approached, unsure whether I would be next and what exactly being next entailed.

If I remember correctly, on Thursday night, I received a list of things to pack but no explanation of where we were going or what we were doing. I was only told to be ready to go at a certain time. The unknown wasn't something I was good at dealing with, and I found my father and

Chapter 21: Jon's Initiation & Blessing

brother to be terrible informants. However, the unknown came on Friday night, large as life.

When we arrived at the site on Friday night, there was a giant tepee and a prepared campsite. It was obvious the weekend was carefully planned. The weekend's events were filled with quiet time, Bible studies about growing up and manhood, and crafting a mission statement. The mission statement I developed is, "My mission as a man of God is to encourage and challenge others to realize their full potential by walking and speaking my truth in love." I was and still am, passionate about digging deep into authenticity and vulnerability while challenging, encouraging, and loving others.

While the daytime events of the weekend were significant, the nighttime events had the most lasting impact on my life. I was led into a tepee blindfolded, then unmasked to find myself surrounded by approximately ten masked men. They removed their masks, revealing the faces of men whom I respect and admire. It was more than a surprise; it was an honor. That night, I gained what many men spend their entire lives searching for, a wise elders' council and support. Through showing up, being vulnerable, and affirming me, the message sent was loud and clear that these men believe in me. As they spoke, their messages confirmed three things I needed to hear: I am loved, they are proud of me, and I am worthy enough for them to invest in me. I also understood they were committed to seeing me grow into a man and were willing to have an active role in my progression.

By sitting in the circle, each man was and forever will be, connected to me—a bond I believe truly transcends time. Since then, I have sought many of the men out for counsel during times of struggle and with questions about God, relationships, and life. Knowing I was a man in the eyes of

Chapter 21: Jon's Initiation & Blessing

my father and other godly men whom I respect has been a rock on which I could fall back on.

For example, soon after my weekend, an older female friend told me I was still a boy. Drawing on that night's events, I was able to confront her and tell her that I was no longer a boy; but instead, I was a young man. I didn't say anything to her about the weekend, so of course, she didn't "get it." Even if I had told her about my initiation, she probably wouldn't have appreciated the significance of it. Either way, it was enough that I knew I was a man.

Her *opinion* was incapable of shaking my *conviction*. My transition to manhood was witnessed by ten men I trusted and who accepted me into their ranks. Most men have to judge their transition to manhood by worldly markers… their first drink of alcohol or sexual experience, or their first time leaving home, for example. Without my initiation weekend and the blessing bestowed upon me, I wouldn't have had any way to refute her attack on my manhood, other than those same worldly markers. My weekend gave me a healthy, godly marker and helped to solidify my identity as a man.

During my college years and into the present time, my relationship with my father has changed from a father-son relationship to one where we are best friends and equals. Yes, there are times where he is still my dad. Still, our relationship attests that we are passionately committed to seeing each other grow in faith, love, happiness, and maturity. I think this passion we have for one another is partially because my father initiated me into the ranks of manhood. He was the one who told me, through the initiation, that we are equals and he believes in me. Instead of having to

Chapter 21: Jon's Initiation & Blessing

spend years of my life convincing him that I was good enough and earning his love and respect, he made it clear where I stood.

Today, he and I can be vulnerable, honest, broken, jubilant, and rebuking with each other, but always with a spirit of love and humility, as iron sharpens iron. I've learned a lot from watching my father closely over the years. I've seen him during times where he's had to dig deep and lean on his faith and character—for example, continuing to tithe when money was extremely tight, sacrificing for the family without complaint while suffering under a toxic boss, and being attentive to and cherishing my mom. Time and time again, I watched him invest his time to set others up for success by providing coaching and mentoring, never shying away from asking difficult questions because he truly wanted the best for them. I also watched him as he worked on himself and as he pursued his goals through I-Group, men's weekends, and applying for different jobs because he knew he was worthy of promotion. His life has been full of powerful lessons for me to learn from.

Below are a few short scriptures that have always struck me as particularly applicable to the initiation and blessing weekend I experienced.

When I was a child, I talked like a child,
I thought like a child, I reasoned like a child.
When I became a man, I put childish ways behind me.
~ 1 Corinthians 13:11 (NIV)

Chapter 21: Jon's Initiation & Blessing

Train a child in the way he should go,
and when he is old, he will not turn from it.
~ Proverbs 22:6 (NIV)

Do not merely listen to the word, and so deceive yourselves. Do what it says. Anyone who listens to the word but does not do what it says is like a man who looks at his face in a mirror and, after looking at himself, goes away and immediately forgets what he looks like. But the man who looks intently into the perfect law that gives freedom, and continues to do this, not forgetting what he has heard, but doing it—he will be blessed in what he does.
~ James 1:22-25 (NIV)

There is much I have left out of my narrative surrounding the events of my initiation and blessing weekend. Finding our way to the campsite, spending the night alone in the tepee in the middle of a rainstorm, my warrior name and the significance behind it, and spilling Skyline Chili all over myself are just a few I have not detailed for you. I also left out the story of the poor froggy that lost his life that weekend. You'll have to ask my dad about the sad, sad story of the poor froggy. Despite my exclusions, you now have an understanding of my experience, the weekend's profound impact, and my relationship with my father.

Thank you to the men who were in my circle that weekend and who continue to support me.

God bless,
By: Jonathan Saas
3/21/08

HonorOurSons.com

Chapter 22
About Jon

After high school, Jon attended the University of North Carolina (UNC) at Chapel Hill, NC. He graduated with Honors, accomplishing a double major by earning Bachelor of Arts degrees in Psychology and Philosophy. As a freshman at UNC, he joined the Air Force ROTC program and entered active duty as an officer in 2006.

Jon has earned a Master of Philosophy degree in Strategic Intelligence and a second Master of Philosophy degree in Military Strategy. Jon has been stationed in various locations throughout the United States and abroad, including four deployments to Iraq, Afghanistan, and Qatar. He now holds the rank of Lt. Colonel. At this writing, he's currently stationed in Dayton, OH at Wright Patterson Air Force Base serving as a Squadron Commander.

HonorOurSons.com

Chapter 23

Henry's Journal About Jordan's Ceremonial Weekend

Saturday, July 3, 1999
1:35 p.m.
I'm on the mountaintop with Jordan. He is at the pond writing his mission statement. I called my wife and spoke to her, Tyler, and Jon. They are going to Cincinnati to run some errands.

I made a pact with Jordan that he can't say, "I don't know." this weekend.

Boy, it is hot and humid today. Sweaty!

2:20 p.m.
Jordan came back to camp. His mission is: "As a man of God, my mission is to be a leader who everyone can look up to, trust, and follow, at all times." He revised his mission statement the next day to read: "As a man of God, my mission is to be a responsible leader who serves others."

Sunday, July 4, 1999
Happy Fourth of July!

6:35 a.m.
I'm ready to go up the mountain to get Jordan. This morning at 1:40 a.m., I was finally alone and trying to sleep in our white van parked in Kent's driveway. I'm not too fond of this part of

Chapter 23: Henry's Journal About Jordan's Ceremonial Weekend

the weekend—leaving my son up there without me. But I must do it. He must "slay the dragon," but I really and truly hate it because I fear for him and don't want him to be alone. These feelings aren't about my son, but they're about me and my ability, or inability, to let go. I must let go.

I got my wake-up call from Jon who was at home since his weekend adventure was last weekend. His call was just in time for me to see the most beautiful sunrise since we moved to the area. I thank God for all He has done to make these weekends the success they were. All praise, honor, and glory go to God!

A picture (more stunning in color) of the beautiful sunrise I experienced after sleeping in my van at the bottom of the mountain. It was Sunday, July 4, 1999, during Jordan's rite of passage weekend.

Photo by Henry Saas

Chapter 23: Henry's Journal About Jordan's Ceremonial Weekend

A group picture of the men on Jordan's weekend.
Jordan, as you can see, is to my right.

Photo by Henry Saas

During Jordan's rite of passage weekend, the mosquitoes were everywhere. I fashioned a bonnet and full-face covering out of paper towels. I couldn't see anything, but it kept the mosquitoes out of my face.

Photo by Jordan Saas

Chapter 23: Henry's Journal About Jordan's Ceremonial Weekend

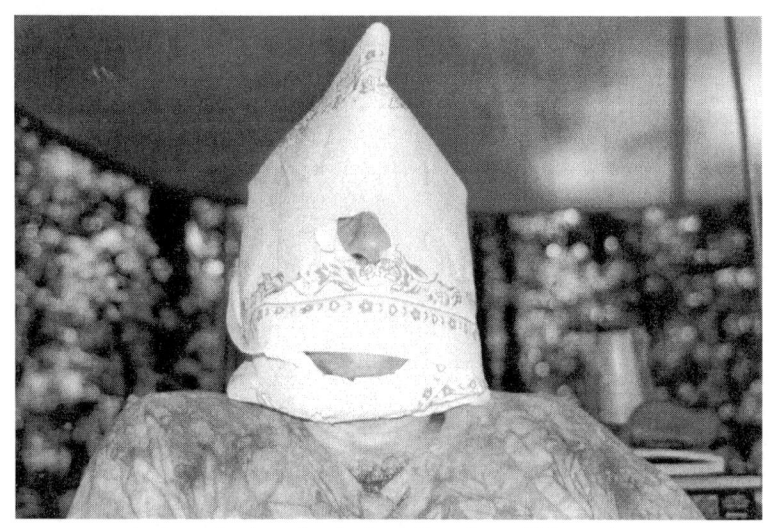

A closer look at the design of my beautiful creation.

Photo by Jordan Saas

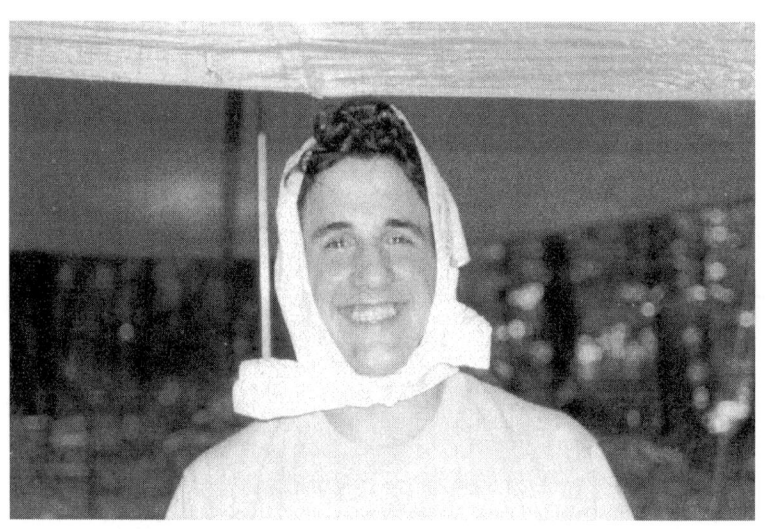

Jordan with the bonnet he made to keep the mosquitoes from buzzing his ears. It was very effective.

Photo by Henry Saas

Chapter 24
Jordan's Initiation & Blessing

But those who hope in the Lord will renew their strength. They will soar on wings like eagles; they will run and not grow weary, they will walk and not be faint.
~ *Isaiah 40:31*

As a man of God, my mission is, "Be a responsible leader who serves others." This mission statement is in my life because of a weekend that will stay with me forever. Not only is it a mission statement, but it's also a passion, desire, direction, goal, challenge, lifestyle, and part of who I am.

I am no longer a little boy who is afraid to step into the unknown. Rather, I am a confident man who takes ownership of the responsibilities placed before him. No longer do I stand in the shadows of my parents, specifically my father. Instead, I stand beside him, creating my own shadow. Just as an eagle soars on the winds of change and adversity, it continues to adapt and overcome to be successful and survive. I am able and willing to do the same. Just as the soaring eagle leaves its admirers standing in awe at its sleekness, power, and decisiveness, I, as a leader to younger men, must teach them to become the same. That is who I am... I am a Soaring Eagle.

I wasn't always like a soaring eagle. Before my initiation and blessing weekend, I was the typical freshman in high school who was ignorant to even the thought of an outside world

Chapter 24: Jordan's Initiation & Blessing

existing beyond the borders of academics, girls, church youth group, and sports. I was selfish. I was oblivious to others' feelings and emotions and the impact my behavior had on their lives. Does my initiation mean I no longer exhibit these traits? Of course not! I am still human. However, my weekend made me more aware and gave me a guideline of how I should—and want to—live out my life.

Since my weekend, I have been placed in many situations where I have had to call and rely upon my mission statement. Some examples of when my mission statement needed to be relied upon include being the captain of soccer teams, Air Force ROTC, Bible study leader, and soccer coach. As I've continued to age and mature, I have also called upon other things, primarily my faith, which you will see in a moment. As a leader, my mission is not only about being a person who is first in line to set the example; it runs much deeper. My mission is to set an example of integrity, service, a bold and courageous character, and unwavering faith.

As I just mentioned, I have called upon my faith to complement my mission statement. Here is why: In the book of Romans, when talking about spiritual gifts, the Bible says, "...if it is leadership, let him govern diligently..." (Romans 12:8c). According to Dictionary.com, the word "diligently" means "constant in effort to accomplish something; attentive and persistent in doing something" or "done or pursued with persevering attention; painstaking." This passage clearly states leadership is not done haphazardly or on occasion; rather, it is done every day! It's a lifestyle.

Additionally, in the book of Colossians, we are encouraged to be men of integrity, "Do not lie to each other..." (2:9). Even more, it encourages us to remain in faith and continue to

Chapter 24: Jordan's Initiation & Blessing

develop faith and knowledge in God's Word. This way, we are not labeled as liars as described in 1 John 2:22-23: "Who is the liar? It is the man who denies that Jesus is the Christ. Such a man is the antichrist—he denies the Father and the Son. No one who denies the Son has the Father; whoever acknowledges the Son has the Father also."

Continuing with bold character... the Lord commands me, as a leader, to be bold and courageous. Just look at the story of Joshua when the Lord calls him to take the place of Moses: "Be strong and courageous, because you will lead these people to inherit the land I swore to their forefathers to give them. Be strong and very courageous. Be careful to obey all the laws, my servant, Moses, gave you; do not turn from it to the right or the left, that you may be successful wherever you go. Do not let this Book of the Law depart from your mouth; meditate on it day and night so that you may be careful to do everything written in it. Then you will be prosperous and successful. Have I not commanded you? Be strong and courageous. Do not be terrified; do not be discouraged, for the Lord your God will be with you wherever you go." (Joshua 1:6-9)

Taking a minute to look at that passage... the Lord tells Joshua to "be strong and courageous" three times! (He also says it again in 1:18 and 10:25.) Repetition in the Bible signifies extreme importance. Granted, the "Book of the Law" refers to the Old Testament law, but the concept can still be applied to the New Testament promise.

What does it say will happen if we are strong and courageous and find our delight in the Lord? We will be prosperous and successful. If you're strictly a New Testament fan, it also states it here: "Be on your guard; stand firm in faith; be men of courage; be strong. Do everything in love." (1 Corinthians

Chapter 24: Jordan's Initiation & Blessing

16:13) Essentially, the Bible tells us to grow a pair (of testicles) and step out in faith.

Service. The best example of service, once again, comes from the Bible. (Are you surprised?) I could spend all day talking about why Jesus' life is the best example of service; however, for brevity, I'll point out the one act that stands out to me the most. It's in the book of John (13:1-17). Go ahead and read that short passage (note the importance of verses 1c, 8, 12-17). I hope it's self-explanatory enough.

The *unwavering faith* part of this story is evident in how I live my life. Jesus says, "I am the way and the truth and the life. No one comes to the Father except through me." (John 14:6) And again, "Remain in me, and I will remain in you. No branch can bear fruit by itself; it must remain in the vine. Neither can you bear fruit unless you remain in me." (John 15:4) And once more, "Everyone who drinks this water will be thirsty again, but whoever drinks the water I give him will never thirst. Indeed, the water I give him will become in him a spring of water welling up to eternal life." (John 4:14) *Why wouldn't you want to have faith?*

In closing, that weekend was life-changing. It was scary to be completely in the dark about my weekend's events, but it only served to prepare me to step into the unknown. It gave me a passion for never-ending service to others. Even more, it gave me a vision to pass along.

Thanks, Dad, for being a visionary and strategic father in a world that lacks so many. Be blessed, men, and continue your journey with faith.

By: Jordan Saas
3/19/08

Chapter 25
About Jordan

Jordan attended Eastern Kentucky University (EKU). He graduated with a double major by earning Bachelor of Science degrees in Emergency Medical Care, and Fire Science and Engineering Technology with a concentration in Fire Protection Administration. Upon graduation in 2006, Jordan started working for the City of Lexington, Kentucky Fire Department as a Paramedic/Firefighter. He is now a Battalion Chief, Paramedic/Firefighter, and the Bureau Commander overseeing the Community Services Bureau. Jordan also serves as the Department's Public Information Officer.

After a few years away from academia, while still working full-time for the Lexington Fire Department, Jordan re-enrolled at EKU. He earned his Master of Science degree in Safety, Security, and Emergency Management in May 2014.

Jordan married Alissa Chase in October 2016. Alissa is a Neuroscience Clinical Nurse Specialist with the University of Kentucky Medical Center. Jordan and Alissa reside in Lexington, Kentucky and have two children.

HonorOurSons.com

Final Thoughts

Congratulations on completing *Honor Our Sons*. Before this journey ends, I want to leave you with a few additional comments about the rites of passage. Furthermore, it is important for you to hear about the lasting impact the weekends had on my sons. This way, you will have a better sense of the potential impact you can have on your child.

Even though my sons are triplets, there were times growing up when they didn't get along. Therefore, I built into the first two weekends an option for Tyler and Jon to serve their brother. After the first weekend adventure (Tyler's weekend), I asked Tyler if he'd be willing to serve Jon by helping me prepare the campsite for him. Likewise, after the second weekend adventure (Jon's weekend), I asked Tyler and Jon if they'd be willing to serve Jordan by helping me prepare the campsite. Tyler and Jon jumped at the chance to serve their brother, to help me, and to revisit the mountain where they had been initiated and blessed into manhood.

An unexpected outcome of their weekend adventure was the importance of their animal names I mentioned in chapter fifteen. These names, Joyous Elk, Wandering Wolf, and Soaring Eagle, became more significant when my sons were juniors in high school. When it came time for them to order their senior class rings, they could pick from a multitude of icons to represent their respective interests and personalities. As they sat at the dining room table, my sons talked about how they would design their rings. They all wanted a cross to represent their belief in God and a soccer ball to represent their passion for the sport. As they were deciding the type of stone for the ring, one of them suggested a transparent stone so they could put the head of their animal name below it. I was moved to tears because one year had passed since my sons were initiated, yet their rite of passage and the honoring of their transition from adolescence to manhood still mattered.

My sons' decision was a reminder that a seed had indeed been planted, taken root, and would lead them to have a positive impact on their corner of the world. Their animal head icon on their senior class ring was a great visual for them to remember their weekend adventure, mission statement, and that they survived an ordeal. Every time one of my sons' friends asked about the significance of the animal icon on their senior class ring, my sons were reminded of the time they became a man.

After each successive weekend, my wife was always glad to see us. She knew the importance of building our boys into men. With that in mind and to her credit, she worked hard to treat them less like boys and more like responsible men. This shift in her behavior required her to go against her maternal instincts as she learned to let go in order to keep a healthy relationship with her sons.

It may sound strange to let go of something in order to keep it, but if my wife or I continued to treat our sons the same way we did prior to their weekend adventure, it would have negated all the lessons they learned about manhood. If my wife and I wanted our sons to continue to grow towards mature masculinity, we had to embrace the new standard. We could no longer enable our sons. My wife and I had to allow our sons to take on more responsibility, and we had to give them more weight in our family by letting their voices be heard when decisions needed to be made. This strategy of letting go helped all of us develop mature relationships with one another.

Final Thoughts

I'll never forget those weekends with my sons. I would like to think their weekend played a role in keeping them out of trouble throughout their high school and college years. My boys grew into wonderful, honorable men. They have achieved more in their 37 years of life than I ever did in my 66 years—and they've done it with integrity. They are loving, kind, grounded, responsible, hardworking, service-oriented, highly skilled in their career fields, confident, and spiritually strong. I could not be prouder of them.

HonorOurSons.com

What's Next?

If you are a mom or dad, and you find merit in my story, take action. In an age where others are constantly influencing our children through social media, celebrities, and peers, we need to do all we can to guide our children into a healthy adulthood. Your first action step might be to make a list of ideas about what you might do to honor your son or daughter. Collecting ideas from key people within your circle of influence may help you, as well.

Will you honor your child into adulthood by creating and implementing an initiation and blessing ceremony for them? If so, will your ceremony be elaborate or simple? There are numerous ways to initiate your child. Will you enlist your friends to help you or plan the ceremony and execute the plan on your own? Are you thinking of initiating only your child or turning your ideas into a group initiation by including several other families? Will you do your part in researching rites of passage? Find out what other parents have done to honorably transition their child into adulthood. Will you slow down to perform mini rites of passage to honor your child for the small, seemingly insignificant life events they have achieved?

Remember, mini rites of passage could be learning how to cut the grass, shave, or drive a car. It might be their first date, their first kiss, serving others, going through puberty, or graduating high school or college... the list goes on. Will you intentionally invest meaningful one-on-one time with your child? What lessons are most important for your son or daughter to learn regarding adulthood? Will you share your story, wounds, and joys

What's Next?

with your child? Are you willing to tell your child what you believe spiritually, including how you came to believe what you believe? Are you willing to be vulnerable with your child while sharing your emotions appropriately?

If you're older and your child is an adult, begin blessing your adult child. If you're reading this book, it means you're still alive, so it's not too late. Start by telling your adult child, "I love you." If this expression of love is out of your comfort zone, begin with mini rites of passage or create a special event to honor and bless your son or daughter. As you go about planning your ceremony and blessing your child, you will also be blessed.

Blessings also work in reverse. If you are a grown child and your parents are still alive, begin to bless them by offering words of affirmation, hugs, saying "I love you," spending time with them, and being a great listener. Oftentimes, the child can be a role model for their parent.

Be intentional. Do your homework. Make and execute a plan. Do it soon. Life is short. Honor your children.

To receive further guidance and support, visit my website for more information and to print off the Appendices.

HonorOurSons.com/Appendices

What's Next?

You can follow me on Facebook under the group name, Honor Our Sons by Henry Saas.

You can subscribe to my YouTube channel, Henry Saas.

HonorOurSons.com

About the Author

Henry Saas grew up in Cincinnati, Ohio. After living for twenty years in the Phoenix, Arizona area, he moved back to the Midwest. He currently resides in northern Kentucky with his wife, Deborah.

HonorOurSons.com

Acknowledgments

Thank you, Mitch, for inviting me to a New Warrior Training Adventure hosted by the Mankind Project (mkp.org). Your invitation changed the trajectory of my life and that of my sons.

I want to give a shoutout to the men who supported me and challenged me in my Integration Group (I-Group). I still work to integrate manhood's noble traits into my daily life as a result of what I learned. Thank you.

Thanks to my Pastor, at the time, for connecting me with Kent and building the Bible study I used with my sons.

To the men who attended my breakfast meeting, volunteered for the site preparation team, and attended one or more of the weekends, you have my deepest gratitude. Thank you for investing in the growth of my three sons by sharing your stories. You made a difference.

To Kent and Lori, thank you for catching my vision and sharing your mountain with my sons and me. It was a gift beyond earthly measure.

To the men in my weekly Bible study, Mark, Steve, and Wayne, and to Brad, James, and Mason who sit in circle with me in our group called B.O.B. (Band of Brothers). Many thanks for your support, friendship, and love.

To my readers, Alice, Brad, Darryl, James, Jo, and Ryan, I am deeply indebted. Your feedback made a significant difference in the quality of my book. Thank you for being readers.

To Lizzy Dye, a talented graphic designer. Thank you for creating the cover design for *Honor Our Sons*. While I thought you

Acknowledgments

did an outstanding job creating the images of a young man, a path, a mountain range, and trees, it was the secret image you cleverly built into the cover design that brought me to tears. During our first meeting, I told you I wanted the cover to communicate that I watched over my sons as they were growing up and as they experienced their initiation and blessing weekend. Lizzy, you beautifully captured my vision. By rotating the cover one-quarter of a turn clockwise, in the last glow of the sun is my profile watching over my son. Wow!

Allison Rimmele, thank you! As my Editor, you exceeded my expectations. The questions you asked and the suggestions you made were spot on and challenged me to dig deeper.

To Terry Sparks, my Production Design Artist, you did a great job creating my Media Kit and posters. Thank you!

To my sons, Tyler, Jon, and Jordan, I'm grateful for the contributions you have made to my life and this book. To this day, I remember the joy and excitement I felt when you and I left home on those Friday nights for our exciting adventure.

To my first wife, Deborah, the mother of our sons, thank you for understanding the significance of initiating our sons into manhood and supporting me through the planning and execution of their adventure weekends.

To my current wife, Deborah, my advisor and best friend, thank you for being a reader, sharing your insights, being open to discuss controversial topics ad nauseam, and encouraging me along the way.

To Elena Rahrig, my publisher, you took my book and turned it into so much more. You captured my passion for guiding boys and men into mature masculinity. You pushed me to

Acknowledgments

share my story, warts and all, for the sake of providing context. Your vision for this book helped us create a teaching tool other men can use to discover the importance of honoring their children. Many thanks!

Finally, to God. You deserve the biggest credit of all. Yes, my friends and I did the physical work, we were your hands and feet, but You did the heavy lifting. You provided the best location and the ideal environment for initiating my sons. You also brought together a team of selfless men who were willing to honor my sons by giving their time and sharing their stories. You performed a miracle right before my eyes. Thank you!

HonorOurSons.com

Appendices

HonorOurSons.com

Appendix A:
Ideas & Insights

Things I want to begin doing for my sons include:
1.
2.
3.
4.
5.
6.
7.
8.
9.
10.
11.
12.
13.
14.
15.
16.
17.
18.
19.
20.

HonorOurSons.com

Appendix B: Important Topics to Talk to Your Son About

Pubic Hair	
Shaving	
Body Odor	
Ear and nose hair	
Going bald	
Dating	
How to treat women	
Love	
Lust	
Masturbation	
Sex	
Conception	
Addictions	
Alcohol	
Pornography	
Drugs	
Gaming	

Appendix B: Important Topics to Talk to Your Son About

Morals	
Ethics	
Social Media	
Friendships	
Peer Pressure	
Educational Goals	
Work	
Career Goals	
Finances	
Politics	
The Value of Life	
Death	
God	
Jesus	
Holy Spirit	
Faith	
Prayer	
Family values	
Ancestry	
Forgiveness	
Self-worth	

Appendix B: Important Topics to Talk to Your Son About

Add your own topics below.	

HonorOurSons.com

Appendix C:
Ceremony and Rite of Passage Ideas

Ideas for My Son's Ceremony and Rite of Passage
1.
2.
3.
4.
5.
6.
7.
8.
9.
10.
11.
12.
13.
14.
15.

HonorOurSons.com

Appendix D:
Men to Include on My Team

List the names of the men you want to include. Mark yes or no for whether they accept or decline.		
Name	Yes	No
1.		
2.		
3.		
4.		
5.		
6.		
7.		
8.		
9.		
10.		
11.		
12.		
13.		
14.		
15.		

HonorOurSons.com

Appendix E:
Breakfast Agenda for Meeting with Potential Volunteers

7:00 a.m.	**Blessing and Breakfast** Pancakes, eggs, juice, water, coffee
7:45 a.m.	**Baggy Items** All men are to empty their pockets, placing all items into a baggy, marked with their name.
7:50 a.m.	**Shoe Dismissal** All men remove shoes to create an "at home, safe" atmosphere.
8:00 a.m.	**Enter Sacred Place**
\multicolumn{2}{|c|}{**For all described below, you will want to record everyone's answers.**}
\multicolumn{2}{|c|}{**Question of the Day:**   What is your mission?   *(If none, put none.)*}
\multicolumn{2}{|c|}{**Introduction:**   Allow each man to introduce himself.}
\multicolumn{2}{|c|}{**Question #1:**   If you were to share one word to describe your relationship with your father(s), what would it be?}

Appendix E: Breakfast Agenda

Question #2:
If you were to share one word to describe your relationship with your son, what would it be?

Question #3:
By a show of hands, who can pinpoint a specific moment when you became a man?

Question #4:
Of those who raised their hand for question #3, what or who told you that you were a man?

Question #5:
If you have had a strained relationship with your father, what's one or two things you most wanted from him? What words? What actions? Both?

Hand out the Information Sheet (Appendix I) and the Needs Sheet (Appendix G).

Thank everyone for sharing and attending!

Appendix F:
Men's Breakfast Checklist

Apple Juice	
Orange Juice	
Cranberry Juice	
Water	
Milk	
Pancake mix	
Syrup	
Eggs	
2 Tubs of Butter	
Pam Spray	
Large Fork	
Measuring Cup	
Ice Chest	
Ice	
Ladle	
Lid to Cover Pancakes	
2 Electric Griddles	

Appendix F: Men's Breakfast Checklist

2 Pancake Flippers	
Rubber Spatula	
Whisk	
Large Bowl	
Smaller Bowl	
Paper Plates	
Paper Towels	
Paper Napkins	
Strong Plasticware	
Extension Cord	
Power Strip	
Playbook: Includes all the notes I prepared for discussion topics.	

Appendix G: Needs Sheet

Musician		
Assign one man to oversee the music.		
What you may want for the music:		
Song Sheets		Guitar
Rhythm Makers		Hand Drum
Site Preparers		
Prepare the site two weeks before the ceremony. When preparing the site, be sure to bless the site through prayer.		
What you will need to prepare the site.		
Rakes	Shovels	Brooms
Firewood		Hay for the Tepee
A tepee isn't necessary, but it perfectly fits my mental image of what I wanted the campsite to look like. It also served to connect this rite of passage to Native American traditions. A tent works just as well.		
First Aid Kit		
Toilet Facilities		
Food Storage (keeping animals in mind)		

Appendix G: Needs Sheet

Water & Cooler
Seat jacks or stumps for sitting
A couple of men to coordinate the potluck feast
Stones for skipping across the pond

… Appendix H: Rite of Passage Schedule

Appendix H: Rite of Passage Schedule

Friday	
9:30 p.m.	Leave the house for the campsite
11:00 p.m.	Lights Out
Saturday	
7:30 a.m.	Breakfast
8:30 a.m.	Hike: Talk of mission and action
10:00 a.m.	At Camp: Bible study
Noon	Lunch
1:30 p.m.	Solitude: Create a mission statement and memorize it. Come up with action steps. Finish Bible study from 10:00 a.m., if necessary.
3:30 p.m.	Snack
4:00 p.m.	Play: Do something fun and interactive. Toss ball, whittle, cook, play chess, etc.
6:30 p.m.	Dinner
9:00 p.m.	Blessing Ceremony Circle of Men: sharing, burning symbol of youth, given symbol of manhood, laying on of hands, blessing

Appendix H: Rite of Passage Schedule

11:00 p.m.	Feast: Food, songs, drums, rhythm instruments, guitars
Midnight	The Edge: Slaying the Dragon. Initiate sleeps by himself.
Sunday	
7:30 a.m.	Breakfast: Pick animal name

Appendix I: Information Sheet

Print First and Last Name
Street Address
City, State, Zip Code
Home Phone Number
( ) -
What gifts can you bring to the weekend?
What do you hope to get out of the weekend?
What weekend(s) will you be able to attend?
Question of the day?

HonorOurSons.com

Appendix J:
Letter to the Volunteers

June 9, 1999

Dear Men,

I continue to need your support, both in prayer and your physical presence. It is difficult to communicate with each of you by phone, so I am sending you this note. I'm sure I'm missing some points, so you may not have clarity with several items, but I'm going to do my best to cover everything. After reading this letter, if you have questions, just ask.

First and foremost, please keep this information to yourself. By all means, you can share this letter with your wife if you desire, but the more people who know, the greater the risk that my sons will find out about this event, making the adventure no longer an adventure.

Below is a list of the men I have approached to help with my three sons' initiation and blessing ceremony. I will refer to the initiation and blessing ceremony as "the weekend."

Pastor	Doug
Jerome	Jessie
Kent	Brent
Bill	Damien
John	Pat
Mark	Monty

Appendix J: Letter to the Volunteers

Below is the list of the weekends and the names of the men who said they could be there. Also listed are the names of the men I don't remember getting a response from. If you happen to be one of them, please call me. Feel free to leave me a voicemail telling me which weekend(s) you can attend. If I have you incorrectly listed, please let me know ASAP.

Weekend #1: Tyler
Friday, June 18, 1999 – Sunday, June 20, 1999
Attending:
Pastor, Pat, Kent*, Bill, Damien
Don't have an answer from:
Mark, Jessie

Weekend #2: Jon
Friday, June 25, 1999 – Sunday, June 27, 1999
Attending:
John*, Pat, Bill, Doug, Monty
Don't have an answer from:
Mark, Jessie, Damien

Weekend #3: Jordan
Friday, July 2, 1999 – Sunday, July 4, 1999
Attending:
Jerome, Doug*, Bill, Monty
Don't have an answer from:
Jessie, Damien

Please notice I put an * by one man's name in each group. This man is the point person. I have not asked the point people for their permission to put them in this role. If you are a point person and do not want to be, please ask someone else in your group to take that responsibility, then let me know ASAP.

Appendix J: Letter to the Volunteers

Attached to this email is a list of all the roles and their explanations, along with your packing list.

It is my prayer to have six men or more at each circle. Please be there if you have committed to doing so, and if you find you can make one that you were not originally scheduled for, feel free to join. It is important to have more rather than fewer men in attendance for two reasons. First, I want my sons to get a sense of the support they have in their community. Second, the more stories you men can share with my sons, the better chance they have of hearing a story that resonates with them.

Don't let the dates of the weekends fool you. You are not needed for all three days of each weekend. I only need you on the Saturday of each weekend from 9:00 p.m. until midnight. I know this time of night is past most of your bedtimes, but God will honor your decision to stay awake.

Attached is the schedule of events for the weekend. As you know, the weekend will take place on the mountain behind Kent's house. For those who have not been there, this event will take place in the tepee on the mountain. If it rains, it will get wet, cold, and muddy, so dress appropriately, for we will proceed regardless of the weather.

I would encourage you to meet at the church at 8:30 p.m. on each Saturday of the weekend you have signed up for, arrange a carpool, leave promptly at 8:40 p.m. for Kent's house (ask Kent for directions if necessary), arrive on site at the tepee no later than 9:00 p.m.

During your arrival and set-up, I will have my son away from the campsite. We will be hiking to the pond and grassy knoll. On our way back, I'll begin a "trust walk." He will be blindfolded, and I will be leading him by the hand on a walk to the

Appendix J: Letter to the Volunteers

camp. As we walk, I will reassure him that I won't let him hit any branches, trip over anything, or fall into any holes. I will explain that it will be critical for him to find a few men he can trust throughout his life.

Men typically don't easily trust other men. I'll continue to explain that men compete with other men in the categories of women, jobs, salary, toys (cars, motorcycles, boats, etc.), workouts, and any number of other things. Most men wear masks and hide their feelings. They might hide behind their work, sports, passive nature, and the like. However, to find men who will share their feelings, get real with you, be there for you when you want to share your feelings, talk through tough decisions, or support you during difficulties in your relationships or your job, is a treasure beyond measure. I'll also tell my son that life is a team sport, and now and then, he'll need to call a few men off "the bench" and onto "the floor" so they can support him. In turn, he can do the same for them.

We will arrive back at the site at 9:20 p.m., which should give you enough time to prepare for our arrival. Please have one man at the door of the tepee on the lookout for us (I'll have a flashlight on so you won't miss us in the dark). At that time, please convert your hushed voices into complete silence and place your masks over your head. When we arrive and enter the tepee, I want him to be confused, i.e., wondering why there is the smell of candles burning when there weren't any when we left. I will place him in the seat of honor, remove his blindfold, and take a seat in the chair located to his right.

I will be the first to speak. I will tell my son that his job is to sit and listen; what takes place is to be held in the strictest of confidence. I will then tell him that during his life, he will meet men along the way. Many of them will be wearing a mask of

Appendix J: Letter to the Volunteers

some sort. It might be the mask of a womanizer, a big shot, a wealthy man, or a mask of anger, fear, hatred, or shame. But behind each mask, it is important for him to remember there is a man with a heart.

At this point, I will indicate for you to remove your masks. If my son speaks as he recognizes you, don't respond (there must be a small degree of hardness at the onset of this process). Your mood should be serious, intentional, clear, and decisive, with strong eye contact with every man you look at, especially my son. Stay focused on the task at hand. Please, no special winks, reassuring smiles, special nods of the heads, etc. There will be time for that after this process. I want him to feel excited, safe, and the presence of God. This request doesn't mean you must look mean or nasty. Convey strength, love, compassion, support, and your love of God to him but do it with your eyes. Be aware of his behavior and facial expressions as his eyes adjust to the light and he begins to recognize each of you.

I will begin by sharing part of who I am and maybe one or two brief lessons that I have learned along the way. I hope I can instill in him some wisdom that will keep him from making some of the same mistakes I did as I was growing up. I won't begin speaking until I have given him a moment to take in what he sees. Be comfortable in that silence.

When I am done, any man who feels moved to share his story/life lesson can go next. I am asking you to share some lessons you have learned as you have grown from boy to man. This portion of the evening might involve a story that has some deep feelings attached to it. Please, please, please, whatever the lesson is that you want to share, I encourage you to take a risk and share your feelings. It has been my experience with men that most of us have experienced shame, guilt, fear, joy, anger,

Appendix J: Letter to the Volunteers

loneliness, and sadness, and when I share my feelings, my worst fear of being abandoned never comes true. Instead, I find myself being loved even more. Share your feelings and share your wisdom. I will support you 100%, as will every man there. This time of sharing will continue until every man who wants to share has shared.

What can my son learn from you about taking on responsibility of becoming a man, a husband, a father, a friend, an employee, or employer, etc.? If you are the father of daughters, express your feelings about boys dating your daughters. Give my son your perspective. As men, all of you are sons, so use your positive and negative experiences of how you tried to relate to your father, friends, and the like.

Most of you are fathers. What have you learned the hard way about fathering or being a husband? If you need note cards to remind you of what you want to say, feel free to use them. However, if it is from your heart, you'll probably do better without them. Remember, if you speak from your heart, you will never be wrong.

Please make your stories about yourself. Don't tell my son what he should or shouldn't do because that makes it about him. Your advice should be from you and about you. His *only* job is to sit and listen. If you need assistance in preparing what you might want to say, seek me out or talk with one of the other men involved. If another man approaches you, I encourage you to help the man identify his feelings around his life. Then talk about it and pray about it.

I am asking each of you to honor one other. Whatever is spoken on the mountain stays on the mountain. Whatever takes place on the mountain is not revealed to anyone. This process

Appendix J: Letter to the Volunteers

must remain secretive in the event we choose to initiate other young men in the future. Confidentiality is paramount! If you can't commit to that, please choose not to participate. I can respect that. This space on the mountain must be a sacred space and safe for each one of us.

After each of us has shared, we will exit the tepee and gather around the firepit. I will have my son take a symbol of his youth to bring with him and put into the fire. We will form a circle around him, and I'll step into the circle and give him a symbol of his transition into manhood. This symbol will be a necklace made of a leather shoelace for a boot. Attached to it will be a small leather piece of cloth that I've tied into a small bag. In the bag will be a small symbol made of pewter that represents an important aspect of his life, i.e., a cross. I will place this necklace around his neck, offer him my blessing, and say a few words about him now being a man in the eyes of his mother, me, and the community. We will lay hands on him and offer prayers to God for this man. When all prayers are complete, I'll close.

The final item on the agenda is to celebrate—have fun, sing songs of praise, eat food (The Feast), toast marshmallows, make S'mores, etc. Then you can go home. Your job is done. I will be leaving the mountain with you and stay in my van for the night, but my son won't know that I'm still on the grounds. From his perspective, I want him to think I left him there by himself for the night. I want to heighten his feelings around the fact that he'll be spending the night alone in the woods. I know he'll be safe, but he won't necessarily know he'll be safe. I call this point in the weekend the "ordeal," also known as The Edge, and Slaying the Dragon.

Part of this ceremonial weekend is much like the blessing of a

Appendix J: Letter to the Volunteers

Knight. If everything were easy, the Knight would have no sense of accomplishment and would have experienced no fear and, as a result, would not have gained courage. I've heard it said that without fear, there is no courage. For a young boy/man to stay alone in the dark woods without Dad to protect him is an ordeal. If my son can survive the ordeal, he will come down the mountain the next day with high self-esteem and tremendous confidence in knowing he can successfully face certain dangers.

What I hope to accomplish this weekend is to have my son walk down the mountain on Sunday knowing:

- His mission statement for this next phase of his life.
- Steps he needs to take to accomplish his mission.
- He is now part of the community of men.
- He is no longer a boy.
- He has special men in his life to whom he can turn for mentoring and support.
- He bears responsibility.
- He survived an "ordeal" this weekend by spending a night on the mountain in the woods by himself, and he was successful.
- He has been honored for who he is today and for who he will be tomorrow.
- He is accepted.
- He is loved.
- Men of God have blessed him.
- I have given him my blessing and support to encourage and guide him as he becomes the man he wants to be.
- God loves him and wants the best for him.

Appendix J: Letter to the Volunteers

This process of initiation is a huge undertaking. I need each one of you to help me because I can't do it alone. The best way to pay you back for all you have done for us is to make myself 100% available to support you if you choose to initiate and bless your son.

Be sure to look for the joy and fun in this process. It's there. Thank you, thank you, thank you!

In His service,
Henry

HonorOurSons.com

Appendix K: Roles Explained

The Point Person
Consider the departure from the church.
Decide as a group if you will make or buy your mask.
Coordinate the potluck.
Assign a man on your team to coordinate the music for the celebration and The Fest.
Keep me posted on any changes or questions. If I am not available, you can check with the Pastor. I have been discussing this event with him in detail.
Everyone (Before the Weekend)
Make or buy a mask to wear.
Cook and bring your dish for the potluck.
Decide which story/life lesson you will be sharing.
Call me if you have any questions or concerns.
Wear weather-appropriate clothing.
Be at the church at 8:30 p.m. on Saturday evening.
Everyone (Once on Site)
Arrange wooden chairs in a circle inside the tepee around the firepit. Place my son's chair in the center as the "seat of honor," located directly across from the entrance of the tepee on the far side. Place my chair directly to his right.

Appendix K: Roles Explained

Locate the candles inside the firepit that is inside the tepee. Light the candles and sit in your seat.
Pray together for God's blessing upon the upcoming event. Ask God to open all our hearts to my son and for my son to be open to the lessons being taught. Please use hushed voices and only speak when necessary. The noise will easily travel in the forest.
Put your mask on and wait quietly for us to arrive.
Everyone (During Tepee Ceremony)
Be ready to share your story/life lesson.
Be intentional, clear, and decisive.
Convey love, compassion, support, and your love for God.
Speak from your heart.
Keep everything confidential before and after the weekend.
Only remove mask upon my instructions.
Everyone (After Tepee Ceremony)
Join in a circle around the campfire, allowing my son to be in the center.
Join me in laying hands on my son to offer prayers to God for this man.
Join me in celebration with music and The Feast.

Appendix L: Sons' Packing List

Sleeping bag	Sweatshirt	Backpack
Long pants (2)	Hat	Clothing for two days
Hiking boots	Face towel	Disposable childhood item
Rain suit	Hot mitt	Pajamas
Flashlight	Toiletries	
Knife	Pillow	

HonorOurSons.com

Appendix M:
Packing List for Volunteers

Flashlight or lantern	
Bug spray	
Long pants	
Long sleeve shirt	
Guitar	
Song sheet	
Rattles	
Drums	
Sticks	
Rhythm maker	
Potluck dish	
Mask	

HonorOurSons.com

Appendix N:
What I Need to Bring

Large water cooler filled with ice water
Large empty ice chests
Large ice chest with two blocks of ice
Six tiki torches and fuel
Dining fly in case of rain
Collapsible camping table
A dozen citronella candles in pots
A dozen candles of various sizes and colors
Matches
Coleman lantern and fuel
Axe
Saw
Shovel
Frisbee
3 Pens
Bandana to be used as a blindfold
2 baseball gloves and one ball
Plastic bowls
Plastic spoons

Appendix N: What I Need to Bring

Plastic forks	
Plastic cups	
Paper plates	
Journal	
Quart of milk	
Reading glasses	
3 spiral notebooks	
2 Bibles	
Battery operated alarm clock	
Box of fire starters	
Ingredients for baking a peach cobbler	
Dutch oven	
2 pairs of working gloves	
Cereal	
Can of bug killer	
Can of bug spray	
Can opener	
Chess set	
Granola mixed with raisins and nuts (trail mix)	
Several lawn chairs or camping chairs	

Appendix O: "What Makes a Man?" Bible Study

How God Defines a Man

At the heart of mature masculinity is a sense of servant responsibility to lead and provide for and protect women in ways appropriate to man's differing relationships.

1. Mature masculinity: Proverbs 15:32 states, "He who ignores discipline despises himself." Authors Smalley and Trent say, "The degree of self-control you have in life is in direct proportion to the degree of the acceptance you have for yourself."

    a. In what areas of life do you struggle most with self-control?

        1. Money?
            – 1 Timothy 6:10, Hebrews 13:5, 2 Corinthians 9:6-8
        2. Sexual impurity?
            – Proverbs 5:3-10, Proverbs 5:18-23
        3. Laziness?
            – 2 Timothy 2:15
        4. Anger with brother or parents?
            – Ephesians 4:26-32

2. Read the following verses and share what you learn:

    a. Luke 22:26 (being a servant)
    b. Genesis 3:9 (male responsibility)

3. Read Genesis 1:28 and 3:17-19 and discuss the different ways a man should provide for women.

4. Describe ways you are called to protect women.

Appendix O: "What Makes a Man" Bible Study

How Women Want to Be Treated by a Real Man
A list compiled by different women shows they want the same things from a man.

1. A man who is honest and can earn their confidence and trust
2. A man who is sensitive and caring
3. A man who is interested in their needs
4. A loyal man who is willing to protect them from those who don't have their best interests at heart
5. A faithful man, never betraying the bond between them.
6. A man whose love is freely given and unconditional, letting the woman enjoy acceptance
7. A man who cherishes the woman, acknowledging her value and importance to him
    a. Compare this list to the description of Christian love below. How many of the six items desired by modern women are on the 2000-year-old list?
        1. 1 Corinthians 13:4
            Love is patient; love is kind.
            It does not envy; it does not boast,
            it is not proud.
        2. 1 Corinthians 13:5
            It is not rude; it is not self-seeking,
            it is not easily angered, it keeps no
            record of wrongs.
        3. 1 Corinthians 13:6
            Love does not delight in evil
            but rejoices with the truth.

4. 1 Corinthians 13:7
   It always protects, always trusts, always hopes, always perseveres.
b. Look back at the list of six qualities that women are looking for. Put a star next to those you think you need to work on.
c. The image of Christ is the standard God imprints on the soul of every woman. She may consciously decide to lower these standards, but it will not be what she wants. Less than the standard will not fulfill her.
d. Look up the following verses and describe the feelings Jesus Christ expressed that are valid for you to allow you to feel like a man.
    1. Matthew 21:12-13
    2. Mark 3:5
    3. John 11:35
    4. Hebrews 5:7-8
e. Read about the mission of Jesus Christ in the following verses and describe how you can participate in fulfilling any of them.
    1. Matthew 20:28
    2. Luke 4:16-21

HonorOurSons.com

Appendix P: Intimacy Needs Sheet

Self	Intimacy Needs	Definition	Other
	Acceptance	Deliberate and ready reception with favorable positive response	
	Affection	Communicating care and closeness through physical touch and loving words	
	Appreciation (praise)	Communicating personal gratefulness with words and feelings	
	Approval	Expressed commendation, thinking and speaking well	
	Attention (care)	Considering another and conveying appropriate interest and support; entering into another's world	

Appendix P: Intimacy Needs Sheet

	Comfort (empathy)	To come alongside with words, feelings, and touch; to give consolation with tenderness	
	Encourage-ment	Urging forward and positively persuading toward a goal	
	Respect (honor)	Valuing and regarding highly; conveying great worth	
	Security (peace)	Confidence of harmony in relationships; freedom from harm	
	Support	Come alongside and gently help carry a load	